JETT

NIGHTHAWKS SERIES BOOK FOUR

LISA LANG BLAKENEY

WRITERGIRL PRESS

Love reading novels featuring hot alpha men who fall for smart women? Then join <u>MY VIP MAILING LIST</u> at http://LisaLangBlakeney. com/VIP and get a free book just for joining!

Published by: Writergirl Press

FOLLOW ME
Follow me on Facebook
Join my Fan Group
Follow me on Amazon
Follow me on Bookbub
Follow me on Instagram

LICENSE NOTE

"Lisa writes books that are intense. Explosive. Panty Melting. Raw. Exposed. Angst. Multifaceted."

"Cover to cover, page by page every word was amazing. This author is amazing and her work is even more amazing. She really can get all the details and words to sound great together."

"As soon as I picked up book 1 I was addicted to this series. I couldn't wait for this one to come out!"

"I definitely recommend this series to readers. It was the first of its kind that I have read, and I was not disappointed. 5 Stars!"

This is a book dedicated to all the readers who can't help but love a quarterback.

Indebted - Cutter & Sloan

Broken - Stone & Tiny

Promised - All King Brothers

King Brothers Box Set

The Nighthawk Series

Sexy & sweet sports romances set in the professional world of football. All standalones.

Saint - Saint & Sabrina

Wolf - Cooper & Ursula

Diesel - Mason & Olivia

Jett - Jett & Adrienne

Rush - Rush & Mia

Freak - Freak & Willow

Brick - Brick & Kaya

Dak - Coming soon

MASTERSON
Meet Alpha Roman Masterson
Free For A Limited Time!

"Our passion is incredibly intense. The connection between us borders on the possessive. Our feelings are absolutely forbidden. The question now is…what the f*ck are we going to do about it?"

DOWNLOAD NOW
Available exclusively through this link.

INTRODUCTION

A one-click, wow he's hot, blind-date romance and big secret love story with the hottest quarterback in the NFL.

From bestselling author Lisa Lang Blakeney comes a new contemporary football romance between a scorching hot pro quarterback and the woman who hasn't got the faintest clue who he is.

A disgruntled pro quarterback with something to prove.

A broken-hearted pediatrician who's lost her way.

An unlikely romance that blossoms out of a chance meeting, a blind date, and one big fat secret.

Jett and Adrienne are the world's least likely couple to succeed.

She's just suffered through the most heartbreaking night of her life.

He's still reeling from the most humiliating game of his.

Their attraction for each other is palpable, yet they have absolutely nothing in common.

Neither of them have the time or space in their hearts for love, but when fate continues to push these two together, will they both take the hint and surrender to a future together or does the secret that lies between them threaten their happily ever after before it even starts?

BEFORE HIM

ADRIENNE

I WAS A FORTUNATE CHILD.

Raised by two parents who were genuinely in love with each other, it was normal for me to see them laugh, hug and kiss each other all the time. To be clear, they weren't inappropriately demonstrative in front of me, but they were tastefully affectionate and everyone could see that they truly enjoyed each other's company and definitely were in love with each other. They were best friends until the day my father died and watching their interaction with each other deeply influenced me. It's probably why I've loved little boys ever since I can remember. I wanted a boy to love me just like my father loved my mother.

I know... it was a complete setup for failure. Let me give you an example.

In Kindergarten, I befriended a boy named Brad Hines. He was the funniest kid in school who always wore a super cool Mickey Mouse ringer t-shirt and had chewy fruit snacks in his lunchbox. He often traded me his fruit chews for my red delicious apples, and I knew it had to be because he liked me. Why else would anyone want an apple instead of those yummy candy-like fruit chews?

It had to be love.

But if it was love, it confused me.

Brad would sit next to me on the class carpet squares during music class but never played with me during recess. We traded our snacks during lunch period, but he never ate lunch *with* me. He cheered me on when we played organized games like Duck, Duck Goose, but he never picked me to be the Goose. Why wouldn't he pick me? It made little sense to my five-year-old brain.

This confusing relationship of ours went on until the end of third grade, when he and his family unceremoniously moved away from New York. They gave the students in the class no heads up about it; so instead I showed up for the first day of fourth grade in my brand new green dress and Brad wasn't there. That would be the anticlimactic end of our friendship.

It wouldn't be until years later that I'd realize how significant the nature of that childhood crush impacted me. As I matured, I realized that Brad only saw me like any other kid in school. I was a classroom friend. That's it. It was me who completely romanticized the relationship because I desperately wanted to mimic what I grew up seeing.

But by this time, the damage was done.

The hurt I felt by his "rejection" of me would take root and become the foundation for all of my relationships with boys and eventually men.

I wanted them to love me, but their actions confused me. I wanted one to be my best friend, yet I didn't know how to effectively communicate with them. And most of all, I expected a man to share his deepest secrets with me, yet I didn't trust them.

Each relationship failure battered my self-esteem, and so I sought to bolster it with hard work and dedication in other areas of my life. I studied hard, played very little, worked out excessively and slept the bare minimum. Even with all of my professional success though, there was one thing that continued to elude me.

Love.

But all of that was about to change.

The moment I met him.

ONE

JETT

IT'S GAME DAY.

The fourth quarter.

And we're playing our division rivals (Philadelphia) in a brutal game. The rivalry is deep and personal for many on the team and fans in the seats. Players are spitting on each other, saying crude things about each other's mothers, and my ribs have just been Malachi crunched by two of the biggest defensive backs I've ever seen.

As I catch my breath, my heart is pounding straight through my chest and the abnormal October heatwave we're dealing with is only exacerbating things. It's hot as Hades out here, the fans are drunk, and I feel the pressure of having to prove something today more than ever before.

My name is Jason "Jett" Caraway, and I'm the starting quarterback of the New York Nighthawks. They are the third team I've played for in four years in the National Football League, and that ain't good. A quarterback who moves from team to team this often is a signal to the league and especially to the fans that I'm a problem. A very expensive problem.

That's why I need to win this game today. If we win, we'll be one step closer to clinching the division, but more importantly, I need to prove all of my naysayers wrong. I need to convince New York that they made a wise investment picking me up in the trade and not a foolish decision.

I can't even believe that it's come to this. Not that long ago that I was the number one pick of the NFL draft. Instead of being known as just another quarterback with a powerful arm, every team looking for a quarterback that year also wanted me for my speed and agility.

I was the complete package.

A coach's dream.

The unicorn.

That year I was at the top of every team's wish list, many companies were lined up to give me endorsement deals, and my agent negotiated an obscene amount of money for me, which at the time was an unprecedented contract for a rookie quarterback.

They discussed my groundbreaking deal on every sports show in the nation; so much so, that veteran players around the league complained. They'd never even met me, but already didn't like me, saying things like I didn't deserve the money because I hadn't proven myself yet. They even said I would ruin the game for everyone if I accepted such an "outrageous" deal.

The nerve of those has-beens. I was the top dog in collegiate sports and deserved every bit of that money. I had proven myself on the field in college repeatedly. Hell, I have the accolades to prove it. I won my university the big championship and broke two of my school's records and one state record in passing yards. Who were they to question my worth?

So I took the deal.

And yes, after I signed on the dotted line, I flamboyantly spent a lot of my paycheck on cars, houses and definitely on women but I'm young and successful and it's my right to spend my money however I want to, right? You would think that would be the case, but the press hasn't always seen it that way. I've been the target of blatantly biased reporting ever since my rookie year. The headlines have been brutal.

Top Draft Pick: Spotted Drunk & Belligerent In Local Bar... Again.

Extravagant Nighthawk Quarterback Hires A Modern Day Butler

Caraway Selfishly Vacations With A Kardashian During Training Camp.

League Admits Caraway Deal Is The Beginning Of A Dangerous Precedent In Professional Sports.

You Be The Judge: Is Jett Caraway A Golden Boy or Spoiled Boy?

Things only got worse towards the end of my rookie year. Through hard work and grit, I got our team to the big dance and playing in my first Superbowl. We had to win a lot of tough games in order to get there, but on that day we were outplayed and out-coached, so we lost. It was disappointing and soul crushing. No amount of money in the world would ever change the fact that I got to the Superbowl and lost it in front of millions of people.

I wasn't used to losing, and whatever their opinion of my personal life, the fans weren't used to me losing either. Losing is not in my DNA, but I'm also a realist and understand that losing can sometimes be part of the game. It happens. Which is why I still don't get to this day, why people only blame me for the results of the game that day?

They said I choked, but I've never choked in a game in my life. They said I wasn't a good leader but conveniently forgot it was my leadership that got us to the Superbowl in the first place. They said I was selfish and immature, but I showed nothing but respect to my teammates and coaches. I always have. I'm Texas born and bred. We come out of the womb revering our elders.

The vitriol thrown my way, especially from some of my own teammates shocked and angered me, and because they hurt my feelings, I reacted and asked the front office to be traded but to my surprise they agreed. I was unceremoniously traded to another team who traded me again two years later.

And now I'm here.

In a city that doesn't want me.

With my previous team, I played under the bright lights under a multi-million dollar dome on brand new turf paid for by the thousands of fans who filled the seats every game, but everything is different with the

Nighthawks. We play in an older stadium on real grass under the sun or the stars, rain or shine.

And the fans are different.

They're grittier, tougher and very dedicated to the team. New York is a big football market and has some of the most loyal and toughest fans in the league, even though their ticket prices are probably some of the highest in the nation.

Unfortunately, those same fans think I'm some sort of selfish, undisciplined, immature, overpaid flop; probably because a picture has been painted through countless media interviews and op-ed pieces that I am. I'm certain that the negativity from the press since my college days has seeped into the consciousness of this entire city.

They've been brainwashed.

And now they hate me.

The overall consensus of the fans here is that they wish management would go with our back-up quarterback, Josh Rivera, instead of me. He's the beloved homegrown veteran from Queens, New York, and I'm the jinxed kid from Texas that nobody believes in.

So you see what I'm up against, right? They're all just waiting for me to make one mistake, and then they'll call for my head on a platter.

I can't let today be that one mistake.

While I may be extremely nervous right now because we're losing this game in a close score, and I just got the shit knocked out of me, I also realize that today is a great chance for me to show the world what I'm really made of.

I'm that kid growing up who arrived to practice early

and left late. I'm the kid who trained twice as hard as anybody else during the off season to build muscle and increase my accuracy. I'm the kid who lives, eats and shits football. It's in my blood, and I truly believe it's my destiny to be the best who ever did it.

That destiny starts now.

TWO

JETT

WE'RE STANDING HUDDLED on the sideline, as I give my offense a quick, motivational speech. I'm not sure how well it's going to work, but it's my job as quarterback to spur my team to victory.

"This game is far from over!" I say with adrenaline running through my veins. "Their defense is getting tired. Let's run the play just like we have a hundred times in practice. Let's get some points on the board."

"Hawks!" we chant in unison.

We get ready to run a play that we've practiced during preseason many times. For once today, my offensive line is protecting me well, giving me plenty of time to find an open man.

As I scan the field, I smile to myself when I notice that one of our best wide receivers, Mark Gibson, is downfield and being held by only one man five inches shorter than him.

Perfect.

The other team has made a huge mistake on man to man coverage. There's no way that dude can hold my receiver. I can toss the ball up high and long, and it's a sure bet that Gibson will catch it.

This is it.

This is my opportunity to turn this game around and I feel it in every fiber of my being.

I step back and throw the ball with precision to Gibson and wait as the ball glides through the air in what feels almost like slow motion. The packed crowd of hometown spectators cheer in anticipation of the catch and the suspense of the moment is palpable. But what I don't see and didn't predict is one of the opposing team's big ass tight-ends running clear across the field in front of my open guy.

It's Wally Mansfield, the bane of my existence. The two of us are from neighboring towns in Texas and products of the same NFL rookie class. He was the highest ranked tight-end in the draft, and we've played against each other many times during our college careers. He is abnormally big, athletic, and fast. No one can bring him down. I mean, it takes like three or four men to accomplish it. If we were on the same team, he'd be my new best friend, but he's not. He never is. Even though we play unique positions, we've been pitted against each other since we were young enough to care about football and nothing has changed now.

Wally stretches his freakishly long arms into the air and intercepts the ball as if I threw it specifically to him, and starts running toward the end zone like an Olympic track star. This dude is a beast. Known around the league for his enormous size and speed, he effortlessly whizzes by my linemen and is headed straight for the red zone to make a touchdown. I see pitchforks in my future.

I feel it before I ever see a thing.

A defensive lineman on the opposing team tackles me from behind and I awkwardly tumble to the turf on one side of my body, face first.

Then I hear a crack.

And then a searing pain wracks every fiber of my being.

"Fuck!!!"

I can hear faint boos from the crowd as the other team runs into the end zone and performs a highly orchestrated touchdown dance. They don't realize yet that it won't count. The asshat who tackled me late is going to be fouled for roughing the passer. Sure enough, it doesn't take long for the spectators to become eerily silent as they see yellow penalty flags thrown on the field and me writhing in pain on the ground.

I see several sets of cleats running towards me.

"Hold on, Jett," one trainer bends down to say. "We're getting the cart."

"No," I say through gritted teeth. "Help me up."

"We don't want to make the injury worse. We're getting the cart."

"No!" I demand again. "Help me up."

Getting carted off the field is not the highlight I want plastered on every sports channel in the nation. It will be a better look if I make my own way off to the locker room with some help.

"You sure, man?" One of my teammates asks. His eyes full of sympathy.

I nod my head yes preferring not to talk anymore in fear that I'll fucking cry.

The crowd lightly claps as two of the trainers gingerly help me up and off the field. I can walk fine because it's my shoulder that's messed up. I pray that it's not what I think it is. A broken collarbone is the kiss of death for a quarterback because the recovery time is so long.

While team physicians numb me with painkillers and proceed with x-rays, the team's quarterback coach, Trent Bantom, sits with me. He's an ex-NFL quarterback and one of the few people in this organization who I believe has never judged me. I respect him a lot.

"This doesn't look good, does it?" I ask him.

His eyes drop. "It's probably your collarbone."

"Is Rivera out there?"

"Yeah, they're on the field now."

"This is absolutely the worst thing that could have happened." I lower my head.

"There are worse things, man. Your shoulder will heal. Been there, done that."

"It hurts like hell."

"It will hurt for a while, but that's not the hard part. The hard part is when it stops hurting and you still can't play because your bones haven't healed. That's when it gets really hard."

"Aren't you supposed to be making me feel better because I'm not really feeling this pep talk, Coach."

He chuckles. "Let's just wait to see what Doc has to say."

About fifteen minutes later, the Nighthawks team doctor comes in the room with a solemn face.

"Painkillers kick in yet?"

"No, I think all you gave me were a couple of Flintstones Vitamins."

The doctor smiles reservedly. "I'll give you some stronger stuff for later because you need to be home to take it."

"So what's the damage?" I ask him. "Just tell it to me straight."

"The bad news is that it's a pretty serious clavicle fracture. The good news is that it's not your throwing arm, so you could come back at the end of the season. It really depends on how you heal."

Dammit.

"I'm going to put you in a sling for now, but you're going to need to see a specialist at Mercy West. He may recommend surgery. They'll probably want to implant some metal rods and screws to help you heal properly."

"What's the minimum time you think?"

"At least six weeks."

I close my eyes in utter disbelief at my horrible luck. I've never been seriously injured before, and now I'm going to probably be out most of the season. What the hell am I going to do?

"I'll be right back with the sling."

For a moment, I forget Coach T is even in the room until he speaks again.

"This could be a blessing in disguise."

My eyes flash open.

"How?"

"Use this time to lie low and keep your name out of the press. No trips to any Caribbean islands. No grandiose purchases. No celebrities in your bed. Just stay under the radar."

For a moment, Coach's recommendation feels like a parental reprimand, but then I remember who I'm talking to and recognize it for what it is, well-intentioned advice and a little tough love.

"I have little choice now, do I?"

"There's always a choice, Jett. The question is, will you finally make the right ones to salvage your career?"

"Salvage?" I feel totally offended. "I've barely gotten started. I don't think my career is in a place where it needs to be salvaged."

Coach T looks around to make sure no one is listening, as if he's not really supposed to be sharing what he's about to say to me.

"This a pivotal moment in your life, Jett. Trust me, I've been there. You think your life is forever set when you're at the top of your game and the money is flowing, but then a life-changing event happens that rocks your entire world—and today is that event. When I was leading the Saints, I went out with a back injury for six weeks and by the time I recovered someone took my slot. Now I'm coaching quarterbacks instead of being one."

"That won't happen to me."

"That's what I said too."

"What am I supposed to do? I've put everything on the line for this team since I've gotten here, and now my collarbone is broken. It's not fair. How can I stop them from replacing me?"

"Nothing is fair about this game. A lot of it is luck, but what you can control is the *other* work you need to do. The internal stuff. Just rest and heal, lie low, do what the docs tell you, and stay under the radar. Don't you paint or some artsy shit like that?"

I nod my head yes. Few people know this about me, but I enjoy painting as a release from the physicality of football. Give me some tubes of Old Holland oil paints and a few brushes and I'm a happy man.

"And quit fighting with the media all the time. Stop giving them shit to write about. The front office will take notice and you'll be more likely to have a job when you're ready to return."

Trent stops talking when the doctor returns and I remain silent myself as the Doc wraps my shoulder and arm in a bandage then rests it in a sling.

Lie low.

Be quiet.

Stay under the radar.

I'm Jason Jett Caraway, one of the most highly recognizable athletes of the year. That's going to be virtually impossible for me. But to keep doing the one thing that I eat, shit and breathe?

I'll give it my best shot.

THREE

ADRIENNE

"ARE YOU ALL RIGHT?"

"Just a kick in the gut," I tell Penny, the nursing supervisor of Mercy West's pediatric clinic. "I'll be fine."

"I should have sent Mary in there with you. She could have held the little demon down."

I chuckle lightly. My last patient of the day is one of my favorites. He's an intelligent little seven-year-old boy with a bright smile and a bad reputation. He hates inoculations and the doctors and nurses in the clinic loathe giving them to him. Every year without fail he kicks someone straight in the gut, and this year I'm the lucky one.

"He's a strong one, but I'll survive."

I finish my last patient chart and hand it to Penny for filing.

"Dr. Hodges, do you have any idea when they're

going to finally transition us to a fully digitized record keeping system?"

"Dr. Hart has a meeting with the hospital to discuss it next week."

"Discuss it?" she says, unconvinced.

"It's a budget issue." I sigh. "In this economy, the hospital has to be careful about any non-budgeted spending. It has to make sense."

"Sure, I understand."

Penny sounds disappointed and I totally understand why. I admittedly feel the same way. The "changes" they promised me were coming when I was selected for a residency in the pediatric department of Mercy West Family Medicine differ greatly from what's actually come to fruition.

I'm in no position to question the system, though. I am a resident who is hoping for a permanent spot with the hospital, preferably here at the clinic. So I keep my head down, I work long hours and pray that I am making a difference for all the little patients that I see.

I check the time on my phone and then slide it in my purse. I'm actually going to make it home early for once in three months. My fiancé, Troy, is going to be so excited to have dinner at a normal hour. We don't technically live together but he spends a great deal of time at my apartment because we both work in New York City but he lives across the river in New Jersey, so it's just easier for him to stay over my place a couple of nights a week.

"You have plans with that sweet fiancé of yours tonight?"

"Yeah, I'm going to cook him my famous chili but with vegetarian ingredients."

"I don't think I've ever had chili. It's not something I grew up eating."

"Well, most folks use ground beef, but I'm going to use the plant-based burger crumbles in mine. It's still delicious and will have a sort of smokey flavor to it."

"Aww, sounds yummy. I'm sure he'll love that."

"Yeah, he's been so understanding about my work hours lately that it's the least I can do."

"I can't imagine how hard it must be to be a resident here and also be in a relationship with someone."

"I will not lie, there are definitely tough days, but I'm very committed to my work and to my relationship. Sometimes I have to compromise or make a hard decision about one over the other, but it all seems to work out in the end. Troy is a very understanding partner and most of all he's my best friend."

Penny sighs. "Maybe that's why I'm still single. That's a hard combination to find."

"No, Penny, you're only single because your Mr. Perfect has yet to reveal himself. He's coming."

"From your lips to God's ears." She chuckles.

"Trust me, I thought after my last relationship that I'd never find the right man, but falling in love with Troy has changed everything. I'm a genuine believer."

"How did you meet him again?" she asks wistfully. "And what do I need to do to meet his doppelgänger? Join a new church? Get on a dating website? Sacrifice my first-born child?"

"I didn't really have a strategy." I smile. "I guess I was just lucky. We have a mutual friend who introduced us. He thought we'd be perfect together, and he was right."

"You are so lucky. It's hard out here for us single girls. Trust me when I tell you should hold on to that one you've got."

I nod in agreement. "I will."

Penny turns toward the file folder cabinet and says, "Have a good night with your Mr. Perfect. I don't work for the next three days, so I'll see you on my next day on."

"Thanks, Penny. Good night."

"Good night."

I dash to the supermarket to pick up the fresh ingredients I need to make my chili. I don't have time to soak the beans overnight like I normally would, so I settle for canned beans instead. Troy won't know the difference. It's all about the seasonings, anyway.

I decide to use my time in the store to check in on my mom. She's been a widower for four years now, and I worry about her sometimes. She's still quite young and could easily date again, but she's just not motivated to meet anyone new. Even in death, she's completely faithful to my father. In some ways, it's a moving tribute of her commitment to him.

"Hi, mommy."

"Hey, sweetie."

"What are you doing?"

"Oh, I'm trying to replicate a recipe I pulled out of my women's magazine."

"What is it?"

"Nothing you would want. It's for marinated lamb chops."

"But you already make a great grilled lamb chop."

"You and your father loved them grilled and practically burnt, but I never did. Just trying to see if I can prepare them a different way."

"Hmm, I didn't realize that you didn't like your chops that way."

"Not a big deal. I'm not that picky about my food."

Huh.

"Right."

"So where are you, sweetie?"

"I'm in the market picking up some things for dinner. I'm cooking tonight too."

"Oh, that's nice. What's on the menu?"

"Vegetarian chili."

"That sounds interesting. I'm sure Troy will like that."

While I am making this dish, hoping Troy will enjoy it, I realize that there's something about my mom's comment that rubs me the wrong way.

"Well, sure, he probably will like it, but that's not the only reason I'm making it. What's more important is that it's the healthier option."

"Of course, dear. You're right. I heard many people lose weight on those vegetarian diets."

I roll my eyes.

"That's not why either, mom."

My mother changes the subject because I get touchy when she alludes to some sort of problem with my weight. I am built very much like my stocky paternal grandmother and not at all like my mother's waif thin side of the family. A fact I've accepted long ago, but one she never lets me forget.

"Listen, sweetie, your cousin wanted me to double check that you can attend her bridal shower."

"Of course I can," I say with an attitude. "I already told her that I was coming."

My first cousin Cecily is the biggest pain in the ass since she got engaged. She is a classic Bridezilla, wanting to control every single part of the planning of her wedding. I have told her on three different occasions through text messages I was confirmed for her shower, but that isn't good enough for her. Now she's getting the moms involved. Our mothers are twin sisters and very close, but Cecily and I couldn't be more different. In fact, we barely tolerate each other.

"Don't get so frustrated with her, Adrienne. The date of the shower is right around the corner and you work a lot. She just wants to make sure that all of her family is there. When you finally start planning your big day, you'll see how much of a monumental task the planning is."

My mom places a slight emphasis on the word *finally*, because in her opinion Troy and I should have planned our wedding a long time ago. Cecily and her fiancé got engaged after us and will be married before us, and she never let me forget that either. I don't think my mom is necessarily embarrassed by it, but she is definitely concerned, especially with my track record with men being what it is.

"I hear you, mom. I will call her so that there is no doubt that I'm confirmed, okay?"

"Perfect. I'm sure she'd love to hear from you."

I seriously doubt that.

"Do you need anything while I'm at the store, mom?"

"No, hun', I'm just going to get back to my chops, then maybe watch an old movie."

"Are you watching anything I might like?"

"I think I'm going to watch Bye Bye Birdie. I haven't seen that musical in years."

"Oh, that's a good one. I love the old musicals."

"Me too."

"Alright, talk to you later, mom."

"Bye, sweetie."

When I pull up in front of my place, I can see my tabby cat, Mittens, sitting in my home office windowsill, which is weird. She normally only goes inside that room when I have to put her away because someone with allergies has come over but maybe she's sitting there because she senses that I'm coming home. Cats are smart like that.

The house is dark and quiet when I enter, and Mittens doesn't greet me at the door as expected because the office door is closed. She must have gotten herself stuck in there unless Troy placed her purposely inside.

I sit my bags down on the counter, slide off my khaki trench coat and work shoes, and open my bedroom door to look for Troy and ask him why he's put my cat on a timeout. Does he do this all the time when he's home alone with her? If so, the two of us are going to have a long talk.

"Troy, why did you–"

Then, like a skidding car that's hit a brick wall, I stop dead in my tracks.

My face painfully mushed up against the glass.

Eyes wide open.

FOUR

ADRIENNE

MY LOVING FIANCÉ, my Mr. Perfect, is buck naked on his knees, serving some woman doggy-styled on my brand new Egyptian cotton sheets. Her facial expression is full of pleasure. His is full of determination. Mine is the look of a woman about to puke all over her hardwood floors.

"What the hell are you doing?!" I shriek in utter disbelief.

Troy's face turns seven shades of red as I watch him internally search for a lie to talk himself out of this.

He mouths the word fuck to himself several times before he stutters, "Let, let, let, lemme explain."

I take a deep breath from my diaphragm and exhale with a long controlled breath.

"You both need to get out of my house right now," I say with deadly calm, before I kill one of them or worse... cry.

I walk over to the long sheer curtains that frame my bedroom window and slide my hand behind one panel. Troy keeps a baseball bat there for my security when he's not here. It's so ironic how this situation could be the first time I may ever have to use it. I hold the bat in my hand and stand at the foot of the bed in what I hope looks like a threatening stance.

"Move," I say, tapping the base of the bat on the floor as I stare directly at the naked woman on my bed. "Faster."

The woman quickly scurries off the bed, grabs her clothes, and heads for the door.

"I'm sorry," she says apologetically. "He said this was his place."

I don't respond to her lame excuses. There are red flags all over this house that would show a woman lives here. She just wasn't interested in acknowledging them. But that's neither here nor there at this point; the real problem is the man I've given two good years of my twenties to.

A complete waste of time.

"You're not moving fast enough," I say to Troy as I raise the bat like I'm on the batter's mound.

"So that's it?" He challenges.

"Is what it?"

"I make one mistake and we're over?"

"You made one hell of mistake, so yeah, we're over. You've got thirty more seconds or I'm going to start swinging."

He holds his hands up in surrender.

"Fine, Adrienne, I'm leaving. Don't bash my head in,

all right? You're going to regret maiming me when you've finally forgiven me for this colossal blunder."

"You've got it twisted. I will *never* forgive you."

I can feel the tears swelling. I need him out of here like yesterday. I cry for no man.

"You just need some time," he has the audacity to say, as if we've just had some sort of lover's spat.

"Leave."

When Troy finally pulls his pants on and leaves my house, I am overwhelmed with feelings of anger, sadness, embarrassment and remorse. I drop like a sack of flour in the middle of my bedroom floor and cry until a phone call zaps me out of my one-woman pity party.

"Adrienne?"

"Hey, Dena."

"Are you ok? You sound off."

I try to quietly sniffle away from the phone.

"I'm fine. It's nothing."

"Don't lie to me. Something is up."

"Well, you will not believe this."

"Try me."

"I just caught Troy in bed with another woman."

There's a moment of silence between us. She's probably just as stunned as I am. We both believed that I had finally found a good one.

"Well, damn, that is definitely not nothing."

"I know," I whisper painfully.

"Aww, Adrienne, I'm so sorry. I know you loved him."

It feels so weird to hear my best friend talk about my fiancee in the past tense already. An hour ago, I thought I was going to spend the rest of my life with him. Now, it's almost as if Troy is dead. Actually, I guess a piece of my life did just die.

"I do... I mean I did love him."

"Do you think that maybe you could forgive him in time? Human beings make mistakes. I suppose Troy is human like the rest of us."

"Absolutely not," I affirm. "They were in my house and my bed. I could never respect myself if I got back together with him."

I tear up again, and a frog in my throat forms.

"Then it's done."

"Yeah, it's done." I sniffle.

"The best thing for you to do to get over a man is to find another one to lie under or on top of," she suggests. "Don't wallow by yourself at home, especially tonight."

"Dena, it just happened."

"Which is exactly why you need to get out of that house. Hell, it probably still smells like sex in there and you might do something crazy like burn your own damn house down."

I glance over at the crumpled bed sheets and almost vomit.

She's right.

There's no way I'm ever going to even be able to sleep in here tonight.

"I think I'm going to burn these sheets."

"And maybe you should in a very responsible and contained way, but not tonight. Tonight you should go have a drink or ten. Get shit faced. You know I'd join you but I've got that meeting tonight and I've already rescheduled it once, but I mean I can if you really need me."

I consider her suggestion while staring at a framed photograph of Troy and I on my dresser. It doesn't take long for me to make my decision.

"Go to your meeting. I'll go to the Wild Boar."

"The old neighborhood spot? I was thinking maybe you could go to the rooftop bar of that new hotel in Midtown. That way if you need to get a room to sleep it off you're just a few steps away."

"I'm not looking to spend half my paycheck on two overpriced drinks. I just want to get good and drunk and forget this night ever happened."

"Okay, call me when you leave there so that I know you arrived home safely."

"It's literally around the corner, Dena. I'm walking."

"Exactly! Some pervert could follow you home and attack you in the stairwell."

"I need you to stop watching Criminal Minds all the time and get to your meeting. I'll be fine. This neighborhood is safe, and I've been going to that bar ever since I was twenty-one years old. It's like that old television show Cheers. Everyone knows me there."

Dena chuckles lightly through the phone. "I doubt that, babe. You haven't been to that bar in a very long time, but okay, maybe you just send me a quick text when you get back home. That will be acceptable."

"If I'm not drunk enough to forget to do it, then agreed."

"Oh my God, who are you and where is my friend who always does the responsible thing?" Dena mocks.

"And look where that got me."

I'm practically in a daze as I peel off my work clothes and change into a pair of jeans and the softest t-shirt I own. I take down my neat topknot that my hair was in all day and let it fall casually around my face. It actually looks kind of nice this way and makes my face look softer and less severe.

All I take with me is a credit card, my ID, and my cell phone because getting to the Wild Boar Tavern is only a ten-minute walk from my apartment.

The plan is simple for tonight.

I'm going to get drunk and try to forget the last two years of my life. Then I'll stagger back home and sleep in for the first time in probably eight months. I've been working nonstop to secure my position at the hospital and to build a bigger life with Troy, but right now all of that seems meaningless.

Tonight, I feel like a complete failure at everything in my life and I'm not even sure how I blundered the test.

Oh, wait a minute, I know how. I trusted Troy.

But the biggest fail?

Was that I dared to trust myself.

FIVE

ADRIENNE

THE WILD BOAR belongs in a 1970s mob movie. It's a throwback bar nestled in downtown Manhattan that desperately needs an interior decorator and some better lighting. They covered the walls in what has to be at least fifty-year-old dark wood paneling and 8x10 pictures of who I think are celebrities that may have passed through the bar in its heyday. Yet with all that said, it's one of the more popular bars in the area. It's tight and loud and not the type of place that you would usually find a medical professional like myself, but this place holds a lot of memories and call me old-fashioned but I'm a sucker for nostalgia.

"Welcome to the Wild Boar. Would you like to sit at the bar?"

A server I've never met before greets me at the door. I think about how I told Dena that this is *my* bar, but she was right, I haven't been here in ages. No one looks familiar except one bartender. The server asks if I want to sit at the bar because that's what you do with people who come to a bar and grill alone, but I don't care about how pathetic I may look.

Hell, let's be honest here, I am pathetic.

"No, I'll take the table in the corner, please."

If I'm going to get shit-faced, I don't need an audience while I do it.

It's so crowded tonight that I need to suck in my stomach as we both maneuver ourselves through the packed crowd standing at the bar and tall-top tables. The server seats me at a small round table near the old-fashioned jukebox in the corner. A Wild Boar treasure.

"This table good?"

"Perfect."

"Do you know what you want to order?" she asks. "Because it might take me a minute to get back over here if you wait."

"Sure, I'll take a basket of chicken tenders with fries and the largest margarita you make with top shelf tequila please."

"Any particular brand?"

"No, just nothing that will give me a headache in the morning."

The server smiles. "No problem. I'll go put in your order and bring you your drink."

I stand up, walk over to the jukebox and smile to myself. They haven't changed the music selection on this thing in years, if ever. Most people are watching the flat screen televisions hung high in strategic corners of the bar, but I want to listen to music, so I press the button for

"I've Had The Time Of My Life" from the Dirty Dancing soundtrack.

I sway my hips to the beginning of the song but become self-conscious as the song apparently increases in volume with each verse. A few people turn around to stare, probably wondering who the nerd is who's chosen this corny old song, so I smile awkwardly but am relieved when they all seem to turn back to their respective conversations.

Everyone except for one very tall human being. Extraordinarily tall.

He's towering above everyone in the room at one of the high-top tables in a baseball cap pulled down low, jeans that fit his ass like a glove, and a nondescript midnight blue hoodie. Standing perched over a beer and a shot of some sort of clear liquor, I can't see much of his face under the brim of his hat, but he's staring right at me with a huge grin on his face.

I'm momentarily distracted by my gawker because of a flash of light from my cell phone. A text has just come in.

Troy: You ready to talk now?
Unbelievable.
Me: Never
Troy: Please, Adrienne.

I suck my teeth, annoyed that he has the audacity to text me after what he's done. I guess my asshole fiancé's actions are finally sinking in his pea-sized brain. Now that the dust has settled, I bet he's realized exactly what he just destroyed between the two of us. I bet if I really wanted to, I could get him to do just about anything to get back into my good graces.

I've had the time of my life
  No, I never felt this way before
  Yes, I swear it's the truth
  And I owe it all to you

This part of the song reminds me of Patrick Swayze holding Baby ever so possessively in their famous dance scene, and suddenly I have an aha moment. I love that movie because not only does Patrick Swayze's character desire Baby, but he respects her, and so the lesson I learned tonight is that there's nothing sexier than respect. Something Troy is incapable of giving.

I can't help but reread the asshole's text message, imagining a variety of sarcastic responses I should send back. Maybe I should send him another one-liner or something intelligent but mean as hell, if that combination is even possible. I want him to be in agony. I want him in pain. I want him to feel exactly how I feel.

I type a few lame words into the chat box, pause, then tap the delete button. I type again, but end up doing the same thing. I can't seem to think straight this sober. None of my texts are mean enough without sounding completely like a heartbroken sixteen-year-old girl.

I need alcohol.

Where's the server with my drink?

"Is this seat taken?"

My head pops up at the resonant voice directing a question my way. It's the same long-legged man who was staring at me a moment ago, but now he's standing by my table and already headed for the chair in the corner before I can even respond.

I catch a glimpse of his entire face under the brim of his hat and *whoa. While* Troy is attractive when he shaves and tries really hard, this man is ruggedly handsome in a very easy and understated way. Even under his sweats, I can see that his chest is broad and probably tapers down to a firm set of abs. His jaw is firm and chiseled and covered in a 5 o'clock shadow of facial hair, and his body language exudes swagger and confidence. Without even trying he has the rapt attention of half the women in the bar and I guarantee you he knows it. He probably revels in it.

"Sorry," I say to stop him, "but yes, this seat's taken."

I've just had my heart ripped out and thrown in the gutter. I am through with men for the foreseeable future, especially ones that look like this. I've wasted two years with Troy and two years before him with another liar. This freakishly sexy man needs to go back to wherever he came from. He's wasting his time over here. I'm not in the mood for casual chit-chat. Maybe coming here was a bad idea.

"Is it really?"

The side of his perfectly shaped mouth curls up in a cocky smirk.

"Um, yeah, really."

"Yeah, but there are no seats at the bar and I gave up my chair for a woman who needed it."

I shrug my shoulders in an "oh well" manner.

"That was very polite of you," I say dismissively. "But you can't sit here."

I feel a few sets of eyes on the two of us but don't make too much of it. I know it has nothing to do with me and everything to do with the stranger. His physical dominance fills the room. The bass in his voice reverberates off the walls. Ovaries all over the bar are probably on high alert.

"I'm not sure I can say the same for you."

"What?" I ask in an irritated voice.

"You're not being very polite."

My eyes widen at how he delivers his straightforward words in the most laid back manner.

"What?" I repeat, because it's the only stupid thing I can think of to say.

"I watched you come in here tonight. You've been here for at least ten or fifteen minutes. You ordered one drink and danced a little to a song. You never turned your head. You never looked at the door to see if anyone was coming. You're alone. There's no one sitting here, not even your purse, and you won't let me sit down?"

"Did you ever consider that I'm waiting for someone?"

"Then they're really inconsiderate for leaving a woman who looks like you sitting alone in a bar like this for so long."

My face immediately softens. I'm a sucker for a flattering remark, especially on the shittiest day of my life. Plus, I notice his arm is in a sling and consider that it's probably hard to drink in a crowded bar with only one good hand. He's right, I'm being uncharacteristically rude. Just because my soul's been crushed by one jerk tonight doesn't mean I have to hate on the entire gender.

"I apologize," I say magnanimously. "Take the chair."

"That's more like it."

I can't help but gawk at my pompous new table mate as he awkwardly maneuvers himself in the wooden chair tucked in the corner. It's a tight fit. This man is not only tall, but wide. Underneath that generous hoodie is definitely a lot of muscle. It's almost as if he's trying to dwarf himself by wearing it, but an impossible feat. I imagine that a man his size with those looks is hard to miss wherever he goes.

"Oh, so you're sitting here... with me?" I ask.

I thought he would just take the chair and sit somewhere else after our uncomfortable exchange.

"Did you order already?" he asks, totally ignoring my previous question.

"Yes."

"What did you get? I'll order another round."

"No thanks, I'm a one drink at a time kind of girl."

He stares down at his beer and his two shot glasses of liquor, then back at me.

"Are you judging me?" he asks with a serious face.

"Umm, no?" I respond reluctantly, hoping I didn't offend the stranger. "Do what you want."

Even with only one good arm, he looks like he could break someone completely in two. But then he throws me completely off kilter by erupting into a fit of laughter. He's actually laughing at me. I'd be miffed if the low rumbling of it wasn't vibrating through my entire body and down to my core.

The crotch of my panties feels cool against my skin.

This is beyond embarrassing.

Check, please.

SIX

ADRIENNE

"YOU'RE the super serious type, huh?" he asks after his laughter slows down.

"Because I don't get your wacko sense of humor?"

"You actually looked scared for a second." He snickers.

Before I can retort, the server returns with my margarita and chicken finger basket.

"Here you go."

She slides my food and drink in front of me but is staring at mister *I'm So Funny* the entire time. My drink is practically sloshing around in the glass, and I have to bend down and take a quick sip to make sure none of it spills over the rim onto the table. She doesn't even ask if I need extra ketchup or napkins as she damn near sits in his lap to focus only on him.

"And how about you, love? Would you like something

from the kitchen or can I get you something else from the bar?"

She's blatantly flirting with him right in front of me and while I understand the attraction, believe me I do, I'm also taken aback. I mean, in another universe this guy could actually be *my* date and she would be acting very disrespectfully. Of course, I live on planet "I don't give a damn" so I let it go. Men are off the menu for the foreseeable future, and if I'm going to be absolutely honest about things, I'm often overlooked or dismissed by people all the time. Why should she be any different?

I have always known that I may not be the first woman people pay attention to upon first sight. Sure, I'm attractive once I've done *all the things* like stylize my hair, put on makeup, wear a nice outfit with appropriate shaping undergarments–and that's ok. I've accepted that. My looks have never been my focus and aren't my superpower. My work ethic is. I wasn't blessed with a genetically perfect body, or superior intelligence, or a lot of powerful connections, but what I am is a hard worker. That's how I got into the medical school of my choice at twenty-years-old and how I've almost completed a demanding and competitive residency earlier than most of my peers.

"You can bring me another round and another of whatever she's having," he says as he hands her his credit card.

"No, that's ok–"

"It's the least I could do for the seat you so graciously gave up," he replies sarcastically.

I roll my eyes. "Another taste of your unusual sense of humor?"

He grins underneath the brim of his cap, obviously very impressed with himself.

"No, I am very sincere about how gracious you are. That must have been a hard decision for you."

"Sure, why not, smart ass," I reply. "I'll take another."

The plan is to get plastered anyway, so I'm sticking to the plan. And why not have him pay for the drinks? I'll consider it the beginning of reparations from his entire gender.

The server noticeably blinks as she looks at the credit card, then slides it in the pocket of her apron. "Be right back," she almost hums her parting words as she switches her hips away from us and towards the bar.

The song I selected on the jukebox played a second time automatically, but has finally ended. Now there's a silence between us I feel the need to anxiously fill with words. Everyone in the bar is talking but us, and since it's clear that we'll be sharing a table tonight, I start with what is easiest for me to discuss, medicine.

"So what happened to your arm?" I ask as I take a huge swig of my drink.

"It's actually my shoulder. I broke my collarbone."

"That's a pretty serious injury," I respond. "How did you manage to do that?"

He pauses for a moment before he responds, as if he's struggling for the right answer. That's a red flag. He's a liar. See, I'm getting smarter already.

"Never mind," I offer him an out. "It's none of my business."

"I got into a fight," he replies.

I scrunch my face.

"A fight? At your age?"

"Sometimes dudes fight."

"Like a bar fight?" I ask, as if that's the most ridiculous thing I've ever heard. "Was it here?"

The stranger looks at me curiously as he slightly lifts the bill of his cap. I get a good look of his other-worldly grey eyes and wonder what secrets lie behind them.

"Umm, no, it wasn't here."

"Oh, good, because if you're one of those guys who gets violent when he drinks, then I'd have to insist that you find another place to sit."

"No, that's not who I am. I rarely drink at all, but I was sick of being cooped up in the house since the injury. There's but so much Netflix one grown man can watch."

I grin and nod in acceptance of his response, although I'm not sure I believe him. I don't like to jump to conclusions about people because you never know what someone's story is, but I'm going to go out on a limb here and call this guy like I see him.

Based on his appearance, my guess is that he's around my age, give or take a year, but is still living in his mother's basement. I bet he's never had to work hard in his life because his looks have gotten him a pass over the years, but now he's struggling. Looks can only take you, but so far. Maybe he gets into bar fights because he's frustrated with himself and thought he'd be more successful by now. Maybe he's one of those guys who thinks life has handed him a raw deal. I wouldn't be surprised if that's him. He basically sounds like half the guys I went to high school with.

"And what happened to you?" he asks, parroting my original question to him.

"What do you mean?" I respond defensively. "I'm perfectly fine."

"I don't know many women who go to a bar and sit at a table alone all night. I'm not throwing any shade, I'm just saying there's safety in numbers and all of that."

I squint my eyes and cock my head to the side.

"You're not some sort of serial killer are you, because I'm seriously thinking that you might just be."

"No," he chuckles. "But if I was, I'm not too sure that I would readily admit to it, now would I?"

"Touché."

I take a bite of my chicken tender. It's piping hot, crispy on the outside and deliciously tender on the inside, just like I remembered. Perfect bar food. Better than sex. Damn, I missed chicken.

"That taste good?" he asks mockingly.

"Like heaven," I reply unapologetically.

"A greasy chicken tender?"

"I haven't had chicken in almost two years, so to me this is nirvana."

He sweeps his eyes up and down my body.

"You're a vegetarian?"

I try not to take offense to his question because a lot of ignorant people (specifically my own mother) readily question me on why my thighs and hips are still so thick if I only eat vegetables. It's a myth that all vegetarians or doctors are toothpick thin, especially when they enjoy French fries like I do.

"Something like that."

"Oh, so you actually *want* to be a vegetarian?" he asks incredulously.

"What's wrong with being a vegetarian? It's great for minimizing chances of heart disease, diabetes, and cancer."

"Right, but I'm curious. What was the one thing that convinced you to give up T-bone steaks and tacos forever?"

"Who said I don't eat tacos?"

"Black bean tacos are not real tacos," he scoffs.

I'll never give this stranger the satisfaction of knowing that I actually agree with him. Black bean tacos aren't real tacos, but that's besides the point.

"My fiancee is a vegetarian, so I became one too. It was just easier to eat the same things."

He looks over at my ringless left hand. I threw my tasteful, two-carat solitaire diamond ring down a sewer hole on my way to the bar. Some might call that stupid, but I have no regrets.

"You're engaged?"

"No."

"Sorry, I don't follow."

I'll never see this man again so I decide that not only will he be my drinking buddy tonight but he can be my confidant as well.

"I caught him in bed with another woman tonight."

"That sucks."

He adjusts his seat, then throws back a shot.

"Yeah."

I swallow another gulp of my margarita and try not to drool at the way he just licked the corner of his mouth.

"I think I understand now," he says. "You're here alone tonight because you need to obliterate him from your consciousness."

Big words from a guy who peaked in high school.

"Exactly!"

This might be the first thing we've agreed on tonight.

"Well, you're going to need some high-quality shots for that. Shots will get you there way faster. These girly drinks you're ordering will make you sick."

"I don't know," I balk. "I haven't taken shots since my first year of medical school."

He sits at attention.

"You're a doctor?"

"Yes, a pediatrician."

"You seem really young to be a pediatrician."

"I graduated high school at sixteen, so I was a few years younger than most of my classmates in college and medical school, but not by much."

"I guess when I think of doctors, I think of middle-aged men with bad comb overs and Porsche's."

"What?" I giggle. "That's very specific."

"The doctors I've seen are mostly men and seem to always be in the middle of some sort of mid-life crisis."

"Hence, the Porsche cars?"

"Exactly."

"You're probably not that off-based, but I work with a diverse group of physicians, so you won't see too many comb-overs at our hospital or at least where I work."

"Wow, your guy fucked up."

"Aww, that's the nicest thing I've heard in a long time."

"I'm serious. You're beautiful and smart, and that's not a combination that most men are lucky enough to find, much less get to marry."

"I guess." I frown.

I didn't feel so smart when I witnessed Troy banging another woman on my bed. How could I have missed the signs that things weren't right between us? There are always signs. I just clearly ignored them.

"So, um, I take it you like Dirty Dancing?" he asks with a devilish grin.

"What?" I ask sheepishly.

"I'm talking about the movie, not the activity."

"Oh, yes, it's one of my favorites from that era."

"That's interesting."

"Why is my movie selection so interesting?"

"Nobody puts Baby in a corner and yet here you are, in the corner, sulking over some loser."

I take another sip of my drink to bury what I really want to say in response to that. How dare he judge me? Who does this guy think he is? I have the right to sulk in peace. He's been doing and saying whatever he wants to all night, and I'm sick of it.

"So what do you do besides fight grown men for fun?" I ask, taking a much deserved potshot at him. "You know for an *actual* living."

He gives me an incredulous look rather than an offended one, and it's the oddest reaction. I can't make heads or tails of him, but that's nothing new. I think the universe can agree that men are a complete enigma to me, and no matter how attractive the man in question may be, I'm determined to keep it that way.

Becoming the best pediatrician I can be for my patients is the only relationship goal I'm seeking from this day forward.

It's the only one that I can trust.

SEVEN

ADRIENNE

"I'M in between gigs right now," he answers somberly.

"That's too bad," I say, giving myself a high five in my head. I pegged this guy correctly from the beginning. "What kind of work are you looking for?"

"I'm just going to take it easy for a while."

He pats his arm to indicate the reason why.

"Oh, of course, the fight injury."

Classic disability hustle. He'll probably file a claim or maybe even sue the man he was scuffling with.

"Did you at least win?" I ask, feigning concern.

"Nah, I didn't."

"That's too bad."

"Yeah, it was." He shifts uncomfortably in his seat. "The chairs are kind of small in here."

"It's an old bar," I explain. "They've had these chairs

since the eighties when people didn't weigh as much." I laugh. "My dad used to go to this bar on Friday nights after work."

"Do you ever come here with him?"

"I came with him twice after he retired," I recollect fondly. "He passed away six years ago."

"Oh, I'm sorry."

He stares quietly at me for a moment, then changes the subject.

"Sunrises or sunsets?"

"Huh?" I crack a smile.

"A little game of this or that. We drink after each answer."

"That sounds a little dangerous."

"The goal is for you to obliterate the douchebag, right?"

"Right."

"This will get you there really fast."

Normally, I wouldn't take part in such a juvenile drinking game. Normally, I wouldn't be out a bar like this at all. I'd be at home studying for the board certification exam while Troy watched something on television. It was a dependable, comfortable existence, but now everything's been turned upside down.

"I'm game."

Anything to forget this day.

"Sunrises or sunsets?" He repeats.

"Sunsets," I answer.

"Drink," he orders. "Now think about the most amazing sunset you've ever seen."

I take a sip of my margarita and think about the red

and purple hued sunset I witnessed while on a Hawaiian vacation. It's the most expensive gift my mom ever gave me for graduating from medical school.

"Salty or sweet?"

"Sweet."

"Good, now think about the last deliciously sweet thing you've eaten."

"This margarita?" I lick some sugar off of the rim of the glass.

"Uh, no, not that," he says gruffly. "Something that made you squint your eyes shut because it was so good."

I think about the tin of brownies a patient's mom brought to the clinic. They were decadent and downright sinful, and I dreamed about those little chewy chocolate squares of heaven long after the entire office devoured them.

The stranger smiles.

"Now drink."

He pushes one of his shots towards me.

"Have this one. The server is bringing us some more."

I hesitate for a moment. I don't really like the taste of straight liquor, but he made a point earlier. If I drink too many of these margaritas, I won't be able to eat for ten days and I've got to go back to work in two.

"What is it?" I ask, killing time.

"It's tequila, the same alcohol that's in your drinks."

"Okay."

I hold my nose and start slowly start sipping on the clear liquor.

"We'll be here all night at this rate," my new drinking buddy chuckles. "Throw it back."

"Ugh, all right. I bet you were a bully in school."

"I didn't have to bully people to get them to do my bidding."

I bet he didn't.

After I finish the shot, he leans over and uses the pad of his thumb to wipe a few granules of sugar off the corner of my mouth. It's the most startling yet intimate thing a man has ever done to me.

"Is he obliterated from your consciousness, yet?"

I blink twice to get my brain to fire up again.

It's frozen.

I think I need to call Dena to come here and extract me from the building, because this jobless wonder is looking even more tasty than he did five minutes ago.

"I want him to be," I say in earnest.

He takes a swig of his beer and grins curiously at me, as if I'm some sort of incredibly unique bird.

"What's your name, darlin'?"

Our conversation is interrupted when the bar suddenly erupts in a unified cheer, followed by some random clapping.

"What on earth is everyone so excited about?"

"The game."

"What game?"

The last time I checked, The Wild Boar wasn't a sports bar.

"Hockey."

"Oh, did the Yankees win the World Series or something?"

He laughs yet again at me, but this time I'm not bothered by it. This time his amusement is infectious.

"What did I say?" I ask, grinning.

"The Mets, not the Yankees, won the World Series *two* days ago. Both are baseball teams, by the way."

"Oh."

"Tonight everyone is watching hockey. The Rangers look good this year."

"Oh," I repeat again feeling a bit like a nerd.

"You don't follow sports at all, do you?"

"Not one bit."

"Not any of them? Baseball, basketball... *football?*"

"No, I guess I'm your stereotypical workaholic type. I don't have the free time or interest to follow professional sports."

"You've never watched them?"

"I just don't understand why adults get paid ridiculous amounts of money to play childhood games, and I definitely don't get why hard-working people spend money they don't have to attend those games or buy the team's paraphernalia or whatever else fans spend their money on."

"Is that so?" he asks, apparently entertained by my response. "Interesting."

"I'm wondering if you truly find me interesting or if that's code for amusing?" I jest.

"How could I make fun of a woman who saves lives for a living?"

This man clearly does not know what a typical day in the office looks like for a pediatrician. It's mostly booster shots and runny noses. The only life I saved today was my own when I braced myself against the knock in the stomach by a seven-year-old brute.

"I take it by your response that you are indeed a big sports fan?" I ask.

"I am."

"I didn't see you cheer for... who was it again?"

"The Rangers, and that's because they're not my team. I'm not from here."

"Oh, so you're a transplant?"

"Yes, ma'm. I'm from Texas."

"Your accent isn't that thick and I think you just threw that ma'm in to make a point."

"My accent is probably watered down since I've spent a lot of time around you, Northerners."

He grins and dear God is that a dimple in his chin?

"I went to Penn State," he continues. "Go Lions."

"You went to college?"

Crap, I hope that didn't sound as condescending as it felt coming out of my mouth. It's got to be that shot of tequila.

I'm definitely losing some of my filter.

ADRIENNE

"SNOOTY MUCH?"

"I'm sorry."

"Yes, I went to college."

"I didn't mean it that way."

"It's fine," he says almost dismissively, and I feel like a Grade A ass.

"No, really, I didn't mean it that way at all. I'm a first generation college graduate myself, and my parents put food on the table every night to pay cash for my tuition. Not one loan. They don't believe in loans, except for their mortgage, of course. I shouldn't of said that to you. It doesn't matter if you went to college or not."

"You're right, it doesn't matter, but just for the record I went to Penn State and you don't need to worry about offending me. I've got a thick skin. Nothing that comes out of a New Yorker's mouth surprises me anymore."

"Oh, so you're one of *those*."

"Okay, now that sounds offensive. One of what?" he asks as he grabs one of my chicken fingers and dips it in a dollop of ketchup.

"Those people from Texas that think they're from the center of the earth."

"One could definitely say the same thing about New Yorkers."

I shrug my shoulders. "I don't think it's the same thing."

"You're from New York, aren't you?"

"Yep, Upper West Side born and raised."

"You come to this part of the city a lot?"

"I don't live in my old neighborhood anymore. I live about ten minutes from here, and while I think New York is a wonderful town, I can see myself living other places. I'm not tied down to living here indefinitely. There's so many other places to see."

When he leans over to steal a fry this time, I watch as his face contorts from what I can only assume is a shooting pain in his shoulder. A broken collarbone is nothing to play with. He shouldn't even really be in this bar.

"I don't know how long you've had this injury, but the fact that it still hurts tells me it hasn't been long. You shouldn't be in this crowded space. What if someone bumps you a little too hard? What if a server spills a drink on you and you suddenly react?"

"I'm getting sicker staying in the house all day."

"There are other places you could have gone. Places that aren't so crowded."

I stand up and walk around to the other side of the table. It's hard not to notice that he's staring at my ass the entire time, and I blush because I can only imagine what it looks like in these jeans. Big. Jiggly. Massive. I'm so used to covering it with my long white lab coat everyday I barely remember what it looks like.

The attention is kind of nice, though. It's been a long time since another man has looked at me like this. Everyone I work with is either old or married, plus when I'm in a relationship I tend to give off unavailable vibes.

"Let me take a quick look," I say as I approach.

"Yes, ma'm."

"You can stop it with the ma'ms, ok? I get it. You're from Texas."

He chuckles again.

He's got the greatest laugh.

I conduct a brief examination of his shoulder and am holding my breath the entire time. From this angle I can closely admire his defined jawline, a small clover shaped birthmark behind his ear, and the tip of what I assume is a rather large tattoo that starts at the base of his neck and ends God knows where.

Whew, there are layers to this man's sexy and lucky is the woman who gets to peel back each layer night after night.

Stay focused, Adrienne.

I bend slightly over to continue my professional

inspection of the injured area, as professional that I can possibly be in a crowded bar of drunk New Yorkers. I can feel some swollen tissue around his shoulder and neck, and then I gingerly try to extend his arm.

"From a scale of one to ten, where would you say your pain level is?"

"Will you make the pain go away if I tell you it's at an eleven?"

I shudder as the warmth of his liquored breath floats inside the cleavage of my t-shirt and settles somewhere below.

"You're an awful flirt."

"Only with women who warrant it."

"You shouldn't be out in this much pain." I say, feeling slightly dizzy by his last remark.

"You've said that already," he says with a smile on his beautiful face, and I need him to really stop it.

"Umm, did you realize that consuming a lot of alcohol isn't a good idea? It will make your inflammation worse. Are you drinking a lot at home?"

"I don't drink at home."

Sure, he doesn't.

He bends forward in his seat and now his face is embarrassingly close to my crotch, so I slowly back away and return to my seat.

"Ok, well if I were you I'd get this checked out again," I say flustered. "Maybe they didn't get your dose right, or maybe you should try a different pain reliever. There are medications they can prescribe to make you more comfortable."

"Comfortable?" he scoffs.

"Yes, comfortable."

"I haven't been able to sleep for a week. I'm way past ever being comfortable again."

My medical residency training kicks in. First, he's in a great deal of pain and second, he's here tonight self-medicating, so I ask the obvious question.

"Do you have access to medical care? Do you have health insurance?"

"You think I'm broke?" he responds incredulously.

"I didn't say that."

Why does everything I say come out sound ass backward around this man?

"What I meant was that plenty of working people in this country don't have major health coverage, and you did say that you were in between gigs."

"Are you offering to examine me for free?" He raises an eyebrow. "Do you do house calls?"

I ignore his blatant come-ons. He's a playful guy. I know he isn't serious.

"I'm a pediatrician, not an internist, but I could definitely find some resources for you."

"Resources," he parrots my words. "This is unbelievable."

"What is?"

"You."

His eyes flicker with emotion. Maybe I've humiliated him? I don't know. I'm just trying to help.

"Because I'm offering you some help? There's no need to be embarrassed about it," I assure him. "This is my job. It's what I do."

"Don't you get it?" he says with ferocity while

slamming his good fist on the table. "You can't make my bones heal by next week. I can't be helped."

Wait, what just happened?

"Um, are we still talking about your shoulder?"

NINE

JETT

I'M NOT SUPPOSED to be here tonight.

Although I'm on the team's injured reserved list, I should still be at the offensive team meeting at Gibson's house, or at home going over my playbook, or between the warm legs of a Nighthawks cleat chaser. What I shouldn't be doing is sitting in the corner of some neighborhood bar and drowning my sorrows after breaking a bone in one of the most anticipated showdowns of the season.

The one thing Coach T asked me to do was to lie low, rest up, and get my personal shit together, but I can't even do that right. I'm not supposed to be hanging out in random bars in New York City. What if someone recognizes me? The bad luck quarterback who just lost the game is now bar hopping? That's how nasty rumors and headlines are born.

To remain incognito, I've come here wearing the

rattiest sweats I could find and I've got my baseball cap pulled down as low as it can go over my eyes, but I'm not positive how well it's working. I feel as if there are already dozens of people in this room who already know who I am. People have been staring at me since I arrived. Hell, I'm pretty sure the server recognized me ten minutes ago.

The credit card I gave her to run my tab is in my non-profit's business name instead of my legal name, but it probably didn't help that it was a black American Express. Not everyone has those. Only people who have a bottomless credit limit and money to pay for it. I'm sure she doesn't run into those regularly, not in this bar anyway.

The way she was batting those five-dollar false eyelashes at me is a huge red flag. I've seen that look before. Her wheels are spinning and it probably won't take her long to figure it all out. She thinks she knows me from somewhere but can't place the face. She's probably wondering: have I slept with him before, did I dance with him at the club last weekend, or did I sit next to him on the subway?

Yeah, I should have left twenty minutes ago.

Yet something about this sexy doctor's heartbroken eyes and spunky spirit is keeping me firmly planted in my seat and ordering another round.

I spotted her the moment she walked into the bar. She's the only woman here who isn't half-naked, bone-thin or slathered in makeup. She's drop dead gorgeous without even trying and has an air of confidence about her you don't see in a woman until they're way over forty.

She's dressed in a casual t-shirt that skims her waist and her jeans are hugging every curve without mercy. She has the most lush heart-shaped lips, breasts that sit close together and heavy, and an ass that damn near makes me want to cry. Her mane of wild curls are thick and begging for my hand to slide inside and grip them at the roots.

I watched mesmerized as she sashayed those luscious hips over to the jukebox and swayed to the tempo of the song she selected before she realized the whole fucking bar was watching. That's when I decided to approach. She was nothing yet everything I expected, which means my curiosity's been piqued. I want to know more. I'm not ready for the night to be over, even though it probably should be.

I stick to a strict regimen during the season. I eat clean and drink very little alcohol, but I've been cooped up in the house for almost a week and I needed a mental health break. I love to paint, but only so many hours a day. I needed a different outlet.

My assistant, Bryan, was not on board with this brief excursion, but I pay him to do the things that I don't want to do, not to have an opinion.

While the plan was to stay under the radar while I was in here, I have to admit that I'm taken aback that she genuinely has no clue who I am. In fact, I'm getting the idea that she thinks I'm some sort of slacker or the goddamn Unabomber. She's not impressed by me at all... and that is some new shit for me. I'm definitely feeling some kind of way about it, especially because she's the kind of woman a man wants to make an impression on.

The attention I received from girls started early because I've always played football. Football is like catnip for some women. The glorious thing about that is no matter your looks, your grades in school, or how well you can dance — you were guaranteed to get the attention of a girl if you played football. It only gets worse as we get older and make money and is probably why most of us behave really badly. We're spoiled, we don't have to work for shit, and the worst part about it is we know it.

Tonight is probably the first time I've had drinks with a woman who doesn't have any ulterior motive towards me. She doesn't know that I'm a celebrity or that I'm wealthy. She doesn't need me to post about her new business on Instagram or lend her some money. We're just two human beings who had a fucked up week talking in a bar. That's it. It's pretty clear that if I plan for her to see me as more than just a lame bar dude without revealing who I really am, I'm going to have to work at it.

Before I can respond to her basically calling me out on my exaggerated response, I take notice of the bells above the door entrance that jingle every time someone enters or leaves. They've been going off all damn night, but there's something about the last chime that makes me glance at the door, and so does she.

She immediately recognizes the person coming in the door and drops one side of her face to the table as if she's hiding. It doesn't take a rocket scientist to figure out why. It's got to be the asshat who cheated on her tonight.

"Is it him?" I ask her.

She silently nods her head yes.

"Lift your head up," I tell her. "You did nothing wrong."

It's clear that this dude has come here for her. There's no way it's a coincidence that the two of them have ended up in the same hole-in-the-wall bar just hours after he banged some chick in their bed, but I refuse to let her shrink in the corner like she has a reason to hide. Not while I'm here.

She reluctantly sits up and takes another sip of her drink, no doubt for bravery. He scans the room in an obvious attempt to look for her, and his face scrunches into almost a painful grimace once he notices that she's sitting at a table with me.

I'm not usually the type to deal with people's personal drama. I'm not going to fight some dude over a woman. There are too many single ones for that. That's why I usually go for the uninhibited, unattached types; women who expect nothing from me but sex and a free dinner. But I'd feel like a total ass if I abandoned her now. She's been through hell and back tonight, and right now she needs a friend.

Her boyfriend is short and light in the ass. He probably weighs no more than a hundred and sixty pounds soaking wet. He makes a beeline for the table, damn near toppling people over to get to us, and I definitely understand why. I don't even know this woman's name, but in the short time we've been sitting together, I already know she's wifey material. And if you fuck up like he did tonight, you better try really damn hard to fix it. Women like her don't come a dime a dozen. She's a keeper.

"Adrienne?"

So that's her name.

Adrienne.

Tumbling out of his pitiful mouth is not how I wanted to learn it, but I'm still glad I know. Her name is elegant and beautiful, just like she is. I can practically hear myself growling it into her ear the first time I make her come.

"What are you doing here?" she asks in a voice laced with pain and tequila.

"I knew I'd find you here."

"How is that even possible? I haven't been to this bar in over a year. Did Dena tell you where I was?"

The boyfriend looks at me, and I glare right back at him. I know silent man speak. He wants me to either excuse myself from the table or explain my reason for being here. I'm not doing either of those things unless Adrienne asks me to. So I stretch my legs out, prop my good shoulder against the wall, and settle in.

I ain't going no damn where.

JETT

"EXCUSE ME, whoever you are, but I need a moment alone with my fiancée," little man says, in a haughty type voice, as if I'm a stack of dirty dishes he needs removed from the table.

"I'm not your fiancée anymore," she tells him plainly.

Good, she sounds strong.

She's got this.

"I'm not trying to have a full-blown conversation in the back of a bar about this. I just need us to talk privately for a second. Let's go home."

I seriously don't like this guy. Anyone with a pair of eyeballs can see that these two would never make it. They don't fit. He's definitely got one of those Napoleon complexes and seems like the type who's insecure about her success. She's a damn doctor, for God's sake, and she still looks fresh out of high school. That he actually thinks the two of them still have a "home" after the shit he pulled tonight is laughable.

"You can't be serious?" She responds.

Exactly.

"Can you give me five minutes outside then?" he pleads.

Say no.

"No, Troy, I cannot give you five minutes or five more seconds because for one thing we're over, and two I'm clearly having a drink with someone and you're interrupting."

Good girl.

I take great pleasure in sipping on my second beer as I wait to hear how *Troy* is going to respond after hearing that. I mean, I've done some questionable stuff to women too, but banging some chick in your fiancée's bed is just fucking wrong. You don't shit where you eat. I think most of us learn that lesson early. This idiot must be a late bloomer.

"Honey–"

"Stop calling me that."

Yeah, that's a totally lame nickname.

"Fine, if this is where you want to hash it out and who you want to hash it out in front of, then that's what we'll do."

That was another passive aggressive request for me to leave, but I ain't biting. A real man would have kicked my ass by now. He doesn't deserve her.

"I don't want to *hash* anything out," she reiterates, but he ignores her like the prick he is and keeps talking.

"Adrienne, first off, all I can say is that I'm truly sorry about everything that happened today."

"Everything that happened?"

She stands up from the table and rests her hand on one of her very ample hips. Damn those hips. I bet he had zero clue how to grab a hold of and rock those hips at *just* the right angle. My dick is getting all worked up just thinking about it.

"You act like it was something that *happened* by some outside force or an act of God," she continues. "As if you didn't cause what happened today. So you're *truly sorry* for bringing a slut into my home and sleeping with her in my bed? That's what you're truly sorry for?"

He doesn't respond right away, but looks over at me for a moment. I can tell that he's uncomfortable and probably humiliated that me and half the bar are now privy to just how badly he fucked up, but that's his fault. If he didn't want to marry her, then why did he propose? If he didn't want to break up with her, then why cheat on her in her own damn house? I'm no shrink, but even I can tell that's some passive-aggressive shit.

It's the stupidest thing to me why so many dudes end up in this sort of position. Stop making commitments when you don't want one. Just be upfront and honest and you can get laid all day every day without the hassle. Shit, I do it all the time. It's so much easier to just be honest. Women love it.

"Yes, I'm sorry."

"Yeah, well, so am I. I'm sorry I wasted two years of

my life with you. I'm sorry I trusted you. I'm sorry I ever met you."

"But we're going to get married, honey. You are my soul mate. Let's figure out a way to work through this. I don't want us to throw everything away over one misstep."

Ok, he's groveling, but he's going to have to do a lot better than this. I give this performance a C minus. He needs to put all the blame on himself and stop with all of this "us" talk.

"Hell. To. The. No."

I lower my hat to keep from laughing in his face after her comeback. I see Adrienne is funny *and* ballsy when she wants to be. I like this side of her.

"I'm only human," he says with his arms spread wide as if he's baring his entire soul to her. "Born to make mistakes."

Wait a minute, did he just quote a song from The Human League? Holy hell, I call bullshit. If the server brings over another drink to this table, I'm going to toss it all over this loser myself.

"If you can't be faithful now, imagine how it will be when we get married."

Adrienne's eyes are a little glassy and I don't blame her. Most women would be curled up somewhere, knee deep in ice cream, and bawling their eyes out after what she's been through.

"Yeah, imagine that," I blurt out.

I did my best to stay out of their conversation, but I couldn't help myself. I hate that she's on the brink of crying. She was doing so well. He should've given this twenty-four hours and regrouped in the morning, but no, here he is ruining my night and hers... again.

Once the tiny man has finally had enough of my interference, he takes another long look at me and cocks his head curiously to the side.

"Yo, do I know you?"

ELEVEN

JETT

"NAH, man, you definitely don't know me."

My guess is that Troy probably watches sports and while part of him recognizes my face, the other part is bewildered by it. This happens a lot when you're a professional athlete.

People imagine we live our lives on another planet. Planet billionaire. Where life is full of the typical over-the-top trappings of success one may see in a movie or music video. So when folks see us in a normal place, like this bar, it confuses them. I'm hiding in plain sight, and his minuscule brain can't compute how a person like me would ever be a part of his average world.

"Well, you're kind of in the way," he says to me. "If you could excuse yourself, that would be much appreciated."

"Can't do that."

"I'm sorry, but what did you say?"

"I said that I can't do that."

"And why is that?" he asks with a firm but guarded tone.

I'm taller and bigger than the average quarterback and definitely than the average man. I'll give him points for not completely folding like a deck of cards, but I can see the fear in his eyes, even though he's trying his best to walk a fine line between "tough guy" and "chicken shit".

"Troy, stop being rude," Adrienne says in defense of me.

"Your *ex* and I have plans after this," I tell him. "And if I'm going to get her home at a reasonable hour, we're probably going to need to get going."

I came up with the first thing that entered my head and it infuriates him, which makes me feel all kinds of warm and fuzzy inside. I watched my mother numb herself with alcohol to escape the pain of my father's philandering. And if Adrienne feels even half of that, I'm fine with not minding my business. Breaking a promise you make to another human being can have devastating effects. My father not only hurt my mother, but I was a casualty of his poor choices as well. I have no sympathy for men who do that to women. In my opinion, they aren't real men.

Adrienne gives me a confused look, but I shoot her a look of my own back, hoping that she understands I need her to play along if she wants to get rid of this loser.

"We broke up two fucking seconds ago and you're on

a date with some stranger in a bar?" He raises his voice at her.

"Watch your tone," I warn him, as the hair on the back of my neck rises. I can't explain my sudden need to protect her, but it's there.

"Is this someone you've been seeing all along, Adrienne?" He accuses.

Typical of the cheater to blame the other person of cheating. I saw this old trick growing up my entire life. It was my father's signature move when he cheated on my mother.

"Uh, uh, uh." I wave my finger. "There's no need to speak to her like that."

"Yo, dude!" he raises his voice even louder now. "This isn't any of your damn business."

Ah, finally the little man has grown some balls.

Several heads nearby turn to listen to us, which makes Adrienne uncomfortable.

"Lower your voice, Troy," she whispers.

"I don't understand what you're doing with this man," he says, in what is now a high-pitched voice that grates like nails on a chalkboard.

Yeah, his balls might be shrinking now.

"I'm not sure you are in any position to ask questions about what I'm doing or who I'm doing it with," Adrienne interjects. "A few hours ago I was coming home from work to make my fiancée a pot of chili and now I don't have a fiancée, so what I do or not do tonight is none of your concern."

"Adrienne, this is not you. This scummy guy you're with is not you."

He grabs her hand, and immediately it makes me want to break his.

"Don't turn into some desperate woman who drinks at bars with strange men because I fucked up."

"I'm not turning into anyone except for the person who I was before I met you... happy."

I'm admiring this beautiful woman more and more as this exchange unfolds. She might have been knocked down tonight, but she'll be damned if she's going to crumble.

She tosses back the rest of her margarita defiantly, slips on her denim jacket and says to me firmly, "Let's go."

When she stands, I follow her beautiful ass like the damn pied piper, but then her ex immediately grabs her upper arm to stop her from walking away from the table.

"Where the hell are you going? I'm still talking."

My patience with this dickhead is fleeting.

"Put your hands on her again and there's going to be a problem," I challenge.

I've had enough of this. There are plenty of ways to grovel without him putting his hands all over her.

"I've definitely seen you before," he says suspiciously. "Who are you? What do you want with Adrienne?"

"Whatever she wants."

Troy scrutinizes me from head to toe as I silently tower over his minute frame. If he thinks I'm at a disadvantage because of my physical injury, he couldn't be more wrong. You only need one hand to land a punch or choke an asshole.

"Adrienne, if you walk out of this bar with this man, then it's over between us."

"It was over three hours ago," she deadpans.

"I'm serious."

"Me too."

There's a satisfied grin on my face when I place my free hand at the base of Adrienne's spine and guide her away from the table and her ex. I'm sure that all kinds of thoughts are running through his head as we leave him standing at the table with his mouth agape. It's all for show but once I noticed Adrienne's lip quivering, I didn't want her to fall apart in front of him, not when she was doing so well.

I stop at the bar to settle my tab.

"Here you go, *Jay*." The server winks and hands me my credit card with a wide grin on her face. If there was any question before, it's clear that she knows who I am now. She probably Googled the name of my foundation on her cell phone and figured it out. "Hope to see you again soon."

I nod a curt thank you, grab my card, and we head out the door. Adrienne never turns back to look at her ex once, and I am oddly satisfied that she doesn't. There's something about the two of us leaving together that feels right.

TWELVE

JETT

WE MAKE a left turn out of the bar and start walking down the street with no clear destination in sight. She still hasn't said a word.

"You can cry if you want," I tell her. "He's not following us."

"I'm not a crier."

"I wouldn't blame you if you did, though. Few women would have been able to hold their ground like you did back there."

"Thanks."

I maneuver around her so that we switch positions as we walk. She's a little wobbly from the alcohol, and I want to make sure that she's on the side of my good arm in case she stumbles.

"Do you need anything? Want anything?"

I'm grasping at straws at this point. I'm not sure what to do or what to say to make her feel better. I don't have any sisters or any platonic girlfriends, so this is uncharted territory for me. How do you make a woman feel better if you're not buying her something nice or fucking her senseless?

"Maybe we just walk for a bit."

I throw the hood of my sweatshirt up to help stay incognito. Most of the photographs taken of me without my permission are mostly of me out and about in the city, because otherwise I'm in my house or at private locations where security is tight and they protect privacy.

"Sure, I can walk you home if you want. You said you live near here, right?"

"I do, but I'm not ready to head home yet."

I forgot that she probably still thinks I'm some sort of serial killer. She doesn't want me to see where she lives.

"Okay."

"That's probably the first place he'll go looking for me."

Ohhh.

"First thing tomorrow you call a locksmith."

"I can't just call a locksmith."

"Why not?"

"I have to call the landlord and ask him to change the locks, and my landlord is hard to reach. It's a whole thing. Don't you live in an apartment or do you still live... at home?"

Damn, I almost gave myself away. Most people our age live in rental properties in New York because we can't afford to buy, but unlike most people in their

twenties, I can. I own a place on the Upper East Side, which I got for a steal at 5.5 million. It was the first major purchase I made once I was traded to the team; it was my way of making lemonade out of lemons.

"That's what I meant," I fib. "First thing tomorrow you get on the phone with your landlord and put in the request for a lock change because Troy is probably never going to give up those keys."

"You don't think so?"

"Not willingly."

"Maybe I should just wait."

"Wait?" I halfway roar because she sounds like she's backpedaling, but then I catch myself. "I'm sorry, I shouldn't have reacted like that. It's your decision."

"You just don't understand."

"What don't you think I understand?"

"I've invested a lot of time in our relationship and he's done nothing like this before. I don't want to make any hasty decisions. I don't want to just throw away two years without thinking things through."

I stop walking and face her with what probably looks like a way too serious look on my face.

"I'm not trying to be a dick about this but I'd bet a hundred bucks that this is not the first time he's cheated on you, and time spent in a relationship is not an excuse to stay with someone who disrespects you."

Time spent in the marriage was always my mother's excuse.

Now, she has no time left.

"Let's talk about something else."

She looks like she wants to puke.

"Sure."

"How's your shoulder?"

"Good," I lie yet again. I'm on a roll tonight. "The alcohol did its job and I don't feel a thing."

"Promise me you'll get a referral for an orthopedic doctor and maybe a pain management specialist. Getting drunk every night is not a treatment plan."

"I promise," I tell her, which isn't a lie. The team already has all of that set up for me on Monday.

She latches onto the crook of my good arm as we walk. I think more than anything she's trying to keep steady on her feet, but the physical connection between us feels nice.

"You mentioned before that you went to Penn State and that you're from Texas, so how did you end up in New York?"

"A job opportunity that didn't pan out so well."

"Oh, gotcha. You know I'm pretty good with resumes if you need some help."

"I'll figure it out," I say, smiling. "I always do."

"How do you spend most of your day? Are you applying for positions online?"

"I paint mostly."

"You paint? What kinds of paintings?"

"I like oil versus watercolor. I'm working on a portrait right now but I'm better at landscapes."

I pull out my cell phone and open my photos app to one of more impressive pieces.

"See."

"This is beautiful. Where is this?"

"A farm in Texas. This is part of the land."

"I'm duly impressed. You really have talent."

I grin so hard I can feel it deep in my chest.

She's impressed, and I didn't even have to throw a touchdown to do it.

"Have you had a chance to see a lot of the city since you've lived here?" she asks.

"Not really. You know how it is. Life gets in the way."

"I totally get it. If I hadn't seen the Statue of Liberty on a field trip when I was in the fifth grade, I probably would have never seen it. There are millions of New Yorkers who haven't visited our famous landmarks. Everyone's too busy and of course no one wants to look like a tourist."

"This might sound crazy, but when I was a kid, I always wanted to stand on the Brooklyn Bridge and look out at the city lights. I heard it was beautiful."

"That doesn't sound crazy at all. Would you want to paint it?"

"Some things I like to photograph or capture on canvas and other things I just want to experience."

"Oh, well, the skyline is amazing from that view, especially this time of year. There's nothing like Christmas in New York."

"Humph, I'm not impressed yet."

"You don't love the shopping?"

"We have bigger malls in Texas."

"The food?"

"Pizza at midnight is getting a little old."

"Central Park?"

"That park is weird. What city has a big ole'

wilderness smack in the middle of it with trees, animals and muggers all in the same place."

"It might be a little weird," she agrees with a giggle. "How about Broadway?"

"Do I seem like the theatre type?"

"I guess you miss Texas." She laughs at me while shaking her head.

"Yeah, I definitely do. Have you ever been?"

"No, I haven't really had a reason to visit. What do you miss most about it?"

"The people, my animals, and most importantly the quiet. I don't think that I'll ever get used to living in a place that never slows down. I mean, look around us. It literally feels likes it's the middle of the afternoon and all these people are still outside. Where the hell are they all going?"

"Nowhere and everywhere," she says as we walk perfectly in tandem. "Just like us."

THIRTEEN

JETT

ADRIENNE'S left ankle teeters and the only reason she doesn't fall is because I've got her.

"Whoa, there."

I pull my elbow in closer to my chest so that we're walking even closer together.

"I didn't think I drank that much." She blushes.

"You didn't."

"I haven't had margaritas in a long time. I think they just hit me kind of hard."

"Yeah, that's probably it."

"So you said you have animals as in plural back home?"

"I have a bunch of chickens, two dogs, two birds, three horses and a goat."

"That's a farm!"

"Back home everyone has lots of animals."

"I bet you're real lonely here then."

"I have one dog with me here in New York."

"What kind of dog?"

"He's a Rottie named Astro."

"That's a cool name."

"He's named after the dog from The Jetsons cartoon."

"I never really caught that one. That's a futuristic one, right?"

"Yeah, I'm a bit of a science fiction nerd."

"Gotcha, aren't Rottweilers kind of aggressive though?"

"No, they get a bad rap. My boy is a big softie. If someone ever broke into the apartment, all he'd do is lick them to death, especially if they gave him a peanut butter flavored treat. He's a sucker for peanut butter."

She laughs, and this time it hits the high point of her cheeks.

So fucking pretty.

"Do you like dogs?" I ask, hoping secretly that she does.

"I like both, but I have to say that in this time of my life, I'm more of a cat person. I need animals that can fend for themselves because I spend so much time at the hospital and the clinic."

I shouldn't even continue with this line of questioning, because I don't want it to slip that I pay someone to take care of Astro every day... my assistant, Bryan. He's probably in my apartment now, feeding him and following up on administrative emails.

"Do you have a cat now or did you just have one growing up?"

"I have a tabby named Mittens." She beams. "She's five-years-old and super cute. My cat before her was a gorgeous Persian named Loretta. I've always had cats."

"I think there's something wrong with people who don't like animals."

She looks toward the ground when she speaks next.

"Troy doesn't like pets."

"Aww, for real?" I say mockingly.

"When I came home tonight, I saw Mittens in the window of my office. For a moment, I thought he had locked her in the room and that perhaps he did it all the time when I wasn't home. I was furious."

"I think that was your sign right there. Wasn't an animal lover on your list?"

"My list?"

"Doesn't every woman had a list of attributes the perfect man should have?"

"There is no perfect man."

"That's the politically correct answer, but that's not really what most women think."

"I can't speak for all womankind and neither can you, but I don't have a list."

"Then is it safe to say that deep down a part of you never completely trusted him? You saw your cat in the window and immediately thought he had something to do with putting her there."

"Only because he's the only other person in my house. That was the logical explanation."

"Would you have thought that if you had left your best friend alone in the house with the cat?"

She pauses for a moment to consider what I've said.

"I think it would have been better if that's all he had been guilty of. What I saw was so much worse."

"I know it seems like that now, but I tell you from experience that it's better you find out who he is now and cut the cord."

"I guess you were cheated on?"

"My mom was, and she paid a heavy price for not dealing with it."

"A heavy price?"

"She died."

We stop walking and she looks up at me with the softest brown eyes I've ever seen.

"I'm so sorry. Losing a parent is hard."

"Yeah, it certainly is."

We continue walking a few more moments in thoughtful silence. I'm thinking about the last time I saw my mom alive, and maybe Adrienne is having the same thoughts about her father. Usually, I grow very uncomfortable when I talk about my mom's passing with anyone, but for some reason it's easy with Adrienne. I'm not sure if it's because she's lost a parent of her own or because she's a doctor and has a soothing bed manner, but it's just... effortless.

"Was it your dad that cheated on your mom?" she asks gently as if I could break.

"Yes."

"And how is your relationship with him now?"

"Non-existent."

"So you don't talk to him at all?"

"Very rarely."

"I would love to have one more day with my father."

"I bet that's because you had a good one."

She nods in agreement. "I definitely did."

"Then you were lucky."

"We're not that far from the Brooklyn Bridge if you want to see the lights," she offers. "The weather will get no better than this until the spring."

Before I agree, I glance over at her again and take a longer look. While Adrienne's eyes aren't swollen with tears, they look exhausted and sad just the same. I'm so not ready for our time together to end, but I realize it should. This night could easily go another direction if I let it go any further, and ultimately she would be the one to get hurt.

"Maybe another time."

"Oh, um... ok."

It might be wishful thinking, but she sounds disappointed that I don't want to go. But looking at the skyline in the middle of the night feels like a very romantic thing to do, and that's not what we're doing here. I wish the fuck we were, but we aren't. A romantic night with me is the last thing she needs after the day she had. It would mess her head completely up.

"Do you have somewhere you can stay tonight?" I ask.

"I can go to my mom's. She lives uptown."

"I'll call for a car."

"That's sweet, Texas boy, but I'll get there way faster

if I take the train. All New Yorkers take the subway. Thought you'd have figured that out by now."

Wealthy New Yorkers don't.

"I just haven't gotten the hang of traveling in that metal centipede. It freaks me out. I rather walk or take an Uber. I prefer to stay above ground. I'll grab you a car. It's no problem."

"Please, I don't want to bother–"

"Adrienne," I interrupt her sentence. "There's no way in hell I'm letting you get on a subway halfway drunk in the middle of the night in New York City. We may not know each other well, but we've shared enough tonight to agree that we're not complete strangers. This is one human being looking out for another after the shit day she just had. Accept my awesomeness."

Then she does something that takes me completely off guard. She wraps her arms around my waist and stares up at me while resting her chin in the center of my chest.

"I accept, but there's just one thing I need from you before we go."

My chest feels like a wind tunnel. A vortex of energy and emotions are swarming around inside, and I take several labored breaths before I can answer her coherently.

"What is it?"

She's so fucking beautiful.

I am dying to kiss her.

"Your name since you obviously know mine now."

Her fiancé almost destroyed her with a brutal deception, but she bravely bared her soul in front of me tonight, so the least that I owe her is one truth. She has no idea who I am and since I have an opportunity to enjoy the anonymity for a few more moments by giving her a name that will mean nothing to her than I will.

I want to give it to her.

I lift the brim of my hat so that she can see the sincerity in my eyes.

"It's Jason."

Then I kiss her once cautiously on the lips and pray that she recalls it in the morning.

It will be the only thing she may remember me by.

FOURTEEN

ADRIENNE

IT'S BEEN seven long days since my breakup with Troy, and I need to readily admit to myself that I'm turning into a crazy person.

You know the type.

When I'm not sleepwalking through work, I spend my time stalking his social media accounts for hours at a time. And I've rehearsed the explanation speech I'm going to give our friends and family about why we aren't getting married in my head about a thousand times. And I've avoided calling my cousin Cecily until I have revised said speech and deliver it without sounding like a wounded animal. And I don't cry, but what's even worse is that I am stuffing all of my feelings down deep with crap that I eat. In fact, this week I've scarfed down three pints of pistachio ice cream, two bottles of red wine and several high calorie dinners via a delivery service.

Tonight I will change things up and cook for myself,

then watch a movie. It's literally a Netflix and chill night and not the kind that ends up with two people rolling in the sheets. I'm eating an artery clogging rib-eye steak, cooked medium, with roasted Brussels sprouts (sprinkled with Parmesan cheese) and a glass of Pinot Noir as I scroll through Troy's profile page like a nut.

Relationship Status: It's Complicated

What the hell does that mean?

I listen to my voicemail for any messages from him, but there's nothing. I check my regular email account and all there is are bill alerts, work stuff and random crap my mom wants me to watch on YouTube.

Don't get me wrong, I don't want Troy anymore, but it would make me feel a whole hell of a lot better if he were begging for my forgiveness. I want him to plead for mercy. I want him to suffer. I want him to freakin' cry. His lack of sincere remorse makes me feel even worse than I already did. Did our relationship ever mean anything to him?

It may not be the most mature thing in the world to want, but him begging on bended knee is what I think I'm going to need to move on from this wickedly painful strike against my self-confidence and womanhood. The two of us have *never* even had sex doggy-styled, and he does that position with a woman on my bed?

I take an almost savage bite of my steak and am disappointed in the taste. I wish it was bloodier. I always second guess myself when I cook things I rarely prepare, and now I've overcooked it. It's well done and chewy. I slam my fork down, disgusted with myself. That's what I get for being a "fake" vegetarian for a man. Now I don't even know how to cook a damn steak.

A tear rolls down my face in frustration more than anything. I feel as if I can't get anything right these days. I even suck at work, which is usually my happy place. I totally missed that one of my patients, a 13-year-old girl, was exhibiting suicidal symptoms and now she's in Children's Hospital with slashes to her wrists. Residents make mistakes and I won't be reprimanded for it, but that's not the point. She could have died and that would have been on my watch.

I wipe the lone tear away with the back of my hand when my phone rings. It's my land line so I know it can only be one of two people, Dena or my mother. Everyone else reaches me via my cell.

"Hello?"

"Where have you been?" Dena fusses immediately on the other end. "I haven't heard from you since last weekend. I was getting worried."

"I've been throwing myself into work every day and then I come home and crash," I give as an excuse. "Sorry about that."

I leave out the parts about my new social media stalking and binge eating habits.

"Have you talked to him?"

"Not since the bar."

"The bar?"

"He came to the Wild Boar that night to talk to me. Were you the one that told him where I was?"

"And break girl code? Absolutely not. I didn't tell him shit."

"I was on Facebook the other day." *Two seconds ago.* "And saw that he changed his relationship status to it's complicated."

"He's totally baiting you. He wants you to see that."

"I'm not so sure about that. He knows I don't really do social media."

"So, he hasn't called you or anything since Friday?"

"Nothing. Not a peep."

"What happened at the bar? Did you two fight?"

"We exchanged a few not-so-nice words. Plus, I was sitting with someone and that only made things worse."

"Sitting with who?" She sounds excited. "Did you bang him?"

"Bang him, Dena?" Sometimes she's so ridiculous.

"Sleep with him. Ride him. Mount him. Hump him."

"Thanks, I get the picture. No, I didn't." I sigh, exasperated. "He's just someone I met. It was really crowded that night and he needed a place to sit, but I think I might have kissed him."

"The bar hottie?!"

"Yes."

"You don't remember if you did?"

"Tequila isn't exactly my friend, but yes, I think I did, and I think I liked it."

"So Troy definitely thought you two were together?"

"I don't know, I might have let him think that. It didn't hurt that the guy was probably the most beautiful man I think I've ever seen."

"Good, serves Troy right. It's kind of odd that you haven't heard from him, though. He doesn't seem the type to easily let go without a fight."

That's what I thought too, but I guess I was wrong about Troy in every single way possible.

"I don't want to talk about him anymore."

"Agreed. He's old news. Plus, I have a great idea for you to get your mind off of things."

"Another great proposition?" I ask sarcastically, because my night out at the bar was basically a total wash.

Maybe I drank too much, but for a fleeting moment I thought that Jason and I had made a connection. A romantic one. I know he isn't my usual type because I tend to attract the regimented, corporate types who make good money and are quite predictable. Nevertheless, I thought there was something.

Troy works in the finance department for the parent company of the hospital—dependable. He wakes up the same time every day—predictable. He eats the same meals every day—boring. He lives a very formulaic life, or at least that's what I thought.

Jason is clearly different. He's drop dead gorgeous, funny, knows how to command a room, and I can tell that he's the polar opposite of rigid and predictable. He's comfortable in his own skin and puts on no airs for people. Something about him is safe yet exhilarating at the same time.

Plus, no one has ever made me soaking wet without even touching me.

I didn't even think that was possible.

I can only fantasize about what it would be like if he actually tried to seduce me.

But when he refused my offer to show him the

Brooklyn Bridge, one of the things on his childhood dream list, it was obvious he wasn't into me. He probably wants to save that for someone special or something to do alone, not with some random sad chick he met at a bar.

Instead, he ordered a car, rode with me home, and hugged me goodbye. He didn't ask for my number or even go in for a second goodnight kiss, because let me say if he had tried, I would have absolutely kissed him back.

Afterwards, when I got inside my house, I felt a little shell-shocked. I'm sure part of the reason was because of everything that had happened with Troy that day, and partly because I was intoxicated, but another part of me just couldn't free myself from thoughts of Jason out of my brain.

Will his shoulder be okay?

Where does he live?

Will he find a new job soon?

If Troy had grabbed me again, what would Jason have done?

Does he have a girlfriend?

Should I go back to The Wild Boar and wait for him to come there again?

I need to stop. I probably dodged a bullet with that one, anyway. I can't date someone who is in between jobs and probably smokes pot all day in his mother's basement while he paints. I shouldn't even be thinking about him or any man. I have more important things to do.

I've got to get my shit together at work, I need to buy my cousin a wedding shower gift, study for the boards, and call my mom back so I can finally explain why I slept over that night then slipped out of the house in the morning like a criminal.

"Go on, tell me. What's the idea?"

"You know my friend Caroline?"

"The blonde from the gym with the best arms I've ever seen?"

"Yes, her. She opened a new business a few months ago, and it's doing really well."

"What kind of business?"

"Get this, it's a matchmaking service!"

"You have got to be kidding me, Dena."

FIFTEEN

ADRIENNE

"I'M HANGING UP," I say emphatically.

"You have something against matchmakers? We watched a whole series about them on Netflix last month. You thought it was a brilliant show."

"That show was for entertainment purposes. None of those people are even together, just like The Bachelor and all those other dating reality shows. They're all actors."

"This is the real deal, though. No cameras. No acting. In fact, one of her matches just got engaged this week."

"It's literally been one week, Dena. Can't a woman grieve the end of her relationship without you trying to set me up every other minute?"

"I know you well enough to know that you're not

grieving, Adrienne, you're wallowing. Those two things are very different. A date is just what you need. If you don't get back out there right away, you might wake up a year from now in a scarf and a housedress looking like your grandmother."

"Excuse you, but my Grandmom Jane is a snappy dresser."

"In the 1970s she was."

"I'm not even thirty yet; I think you're dramatizing the situation."

"That's exactly how it happens. Look at my sister. She's forty and living with her baby's daddy because she farted around for twenty years and then settled for the only guy around when she was ready to have a baby."

"Maybe her relationship makes her happy. Everyone isn't going to find their perfect match like you and Danny. "

Dena is my day one. My best friend. She fell in love with Danny in the sixth grade, and neither of them have ever looked at anyone else since. After college, the two of them started a small nonprofit organization that helps men find work after being released from prison. Danny spends most of his time with outreach to prisons and Dena spends most of her time applying for grants and finding businesses who will hire felons. Their life could literally be a Hallmark movie. It's inspiring, romantic and disgusting all rolled into one, and it has also unofficially made her our friend group's go-to relationship expert.

A role she relishes.

"Just go on one date."

"Not interested."

"She only deals with a certain clientele. The men have to pay a lot of money to join so you know they're serious."

"Exactly my point, I don't want anything serious."

"Of course not, but at least you won't be dating someone whose only agenda is to get inside your pants."

"The perfect solution for that would be abstinence."

"Don't give Troy the satisfaction of knowing that you're miserable without him."

"I'm not miserable without him," I protest. "I'm miserable *because* of him."

"So we agree then?"

"I see why your organization is so successful. You don't take no for an answer."

"I'm allergic to that word. You of all people should know that about me."

"You're never going to stop are you?" I ask, already exhausted by this conversation.

"You're my best friend and it's my duty to help you find happiness, especially when an opportunity like this falls on my lap."

"How much is this opportunity? You know I'm on a budget."

"Dang, you're the most broke doctor I've ever met," she snorts.

"I should have been a plastic surgeon, but alas, I love the children."

Dena giggles. "For you, bestie, I have arranged for the match to be free. The only catch is that you're going to have to go on three dates. You can't bail after just one."

"You mean I can't quit after seeing what a complete waste of time this will be?"

"Caroline has studied statistics on arranged relationships and they have a better chance of working given adequate time to become invested in the other person. It's just that the first date is always the hardest, because people often make assumptions and judgments based on a brief first impression. Give the process time."

"I can't commit to three dates. I've got work and my boards coming up."

"I need you to trust the process."

"Dammit," I hear my cell phone vibrating on the counter. "Cecily is calling me."

"Pick it up and use me as an excuse to get off the phone."

"Okay, hold on."

"Hello?"

"Adrienne freaking Hodges!"

"Hey, Cecily." I use my fake happy to hear from her voice.

"I've been trying to get a hold of you for the longest time."

"I'm so sorry. You know how it is. Work and everything."

"Mommy mentioned you were working long hours and stuff. You're still a resident, right? You know, I don't know the difference. When do you become a real doctor?"

Her question irks the hell out of me, which I'm sure was her intention.

"I already am an actual doctor," I say plainly. "A

residency just means that I'm still training in my specialty under the senior physicians at the hospital."

"Oh, that's right."

My cousin can be a Grade A bitch when she wants. She's so passive aggressive it's sickening, and my mom doesn't see it at all. She loves her niece about as much as she loves me, sometimes I think even more.

"Listen, I'm on the other line, but I know you're calling about the shower. I responded weeks ago."

"You sent a text, so I wasn't sure."

You weren't sure about the text that read: I will attend?

"I'm coming." I say matter-of-factly. "I wouldn't miss it."

"Fantastic, I'll seat you next to my sorority sisters. I want you to get to know them better."

"Uh-huh, great."

"So, how's my boy Troy doing?"

Cecily thinks Troy is the greatest thing since sliced bread, but that's what she thought about my last boyfriend too. That must be the one thing we have in common, a terrible judge of character.

"He's good. Look, I gotta go," I cut off the conversation. "I'm on the other line with Dena. I'll call you later."

"Oh," she sounds flustered by my abruptness, but this is the only way to deal with Cecily. Politeness gets you nowhere but on the phone for thirty minutes longer than you ever wanted to be. "Okay, tell her I said hi and if I don't talk to you before then I'll see you at the shower. Remember, the color theme is blush pink."

Color theme?

Jesus Christ.

"Sure, got it."

I hang up before she tells me anything else and get back to my conversation with Dena.

"I'm back."

"I bet you can't wait for this wedding to be over."

"Amen."

"I'm still a little hurt that she invited me and Danny to the wedding but didn't invite me to the shower. What kind of hellish mess is that?"

"You want me to ask her?"

"Definitely not, I don't even want to go. It's just a point I'm making. I've known Cecily since we were seven-years-old and I don't make the cut?"

"I am starting to truly believe that you see a person's true colors emerge once they plan a wedding. It's probably the reason I never started planning mine. The stress to get it all right feels overwhelming."

"Oh, I know! Maybe your blind date guy can go to the wedding with you."

"I'm a very busy woman who just got out of a long-term relationship and you want me to go on three dates with a stranger and take him to a family wedding?"

"Three dates and a wee promise to do a video testimonial if the dates are good."

"A video testimonial!"

"Just one." Her voice shrinks on the phone.

"How many other *wee* promises did you make on my behalf? My first-born son?"

"If you want to name him after me when this works out, I wouldn't mind."

I snort at that lame response.

"What's in it for you?"

"Besides the blissful happiness of my dearest friend?"

"Uh, yeah," I say suspiciously. "There's got to be something else."

"Okay, real talk, Catherine is already loaded. She lives off a trust her grandfather created for her. She doesn't need this business to work, but she's promised to fund a six-figure grant for us with a commitment of three years if I can make this happen."

"Why me?"

"She wants to be able to say that women who are physicians are part of her clientele. It's important that certain types of people are in the applicant pool."

"Finally, the truth. This whole thing is just some rich girl's hobby to pass the time."

"A rich girl whose help your best friend needs."

My cell phone vibrates again. I'm going to scream if it's Cecily, but it isn't her. It's a text from Troy. The first one he's sent in seven days.

Troy: Have you calmed down yet?

After a week, that's the first thing he has to say to me? What a complete asshole.

I furiously search for the right emoji to send in response as I continue my conversation with Dena. Where is that damn middle finger emoji?

"Set it up, Dena."

"Really?" she asks excitedly. "You'll go on all three of

the dates? They promised to work around your schedule and–"

I cut off her sales pitch.

"I'll do it."

I decide Troy's ridiculous text warrants more than an angry emoji, so I hit send on my short and plain response. It describes exactly how I feel.

Me: Go. Kick. Rocks.

JETT

"THIS SMOOTHIE TASTES LIKE SEAWATER."

"And good morning to you too."

I pour a little of it on the floor to see if Astro will eat it.

"You want some of this, boy?"

My big boy saunters over, takes a few whiffs and casually returns to his king sized bean bag without as much as a lick.

"See, even Astro won't drink it."

My mood stinks because I'm exhausted. I spent half the night having the craziest dreams, and the universe saw fit to allow me to remember a few. Adrienne was in each and every one of them. I know that it's simply my subconscious fucking with me. I should have gotten her number. I should have gone in for the goodnight kiss. I know where she lives, but if I looked her up, there is no doubt that she would probably get a restraining order on my ass. I would definitely come off like some sort of creeper. So, I have to let it go, but regrets are the unwanted bedfellow of the unfulfilled mind. In other words, this shit is going to fuck with me for a minute.

"Make me another one."

"Jett, I make the same smoothie for you every morning," Brad says. "There's nothing different in it."

"Make me another one, *please*."

My assistant sighs heavily.

"What's your deal this morning?"

"The deal is my shoulder's shattered, I can't sleep, and I'm not playing football."

"And that's it?"

"Isn't that enough?"

"Fine, Jett, I'll go make another smoothie, but you better drink it. You can't take the pain meds on an empty stomach."

Bryan is only three years younger than me but has the patience of a saint. He babysits me, walks and feeds Astro, maintains my schedule, and handles some administrative emails of the non-profit foundation I created in honor of my mother.

I know I'm a pain in the ass, but I've already warned him I feel like a caged animal and will probably be annoying until I can play again. I'm used to a day of training or playing ball until I'm completely exhausted, maybe having some sex, and then crashing until the morning. None of that is going on right now. I can't play ball because of my shoulder, and I definitely can't fuck someone properly when I keep having dreams about a woman I met in a bar over a week ago.

"By the way your pop called," Bryan mentions.

"What did he want?"

"He said he just wanted to check in on you and your shoulder. See how you were feeling."

"He wanted to make sure his paycheck was still coming. He can't support that new wife and kid of his without it. Nobody told him to move to a place where the cost of living is ridiculously high."

"I'm sure the fact that you live in New York too is a big part of the move."

"It's just a coincidence. His new lady is from New York. That's why they moved back here."

"Well, I think he's smart enough to realize that you can pay his bills regardless if you play another game or not. His call to check in sounded genuine."

"I don't pay you for family counseling, Young Padawan."

Padawan is my Star Wars nickname for Bryan. I'm the Jedi Master, and he's my young Padawan. Yeah, we're science fiction nerds like that. If I didn't play football, I'd probably be in art school studying to be animation artist.

"Fine, I'm just saying, I thought you enjoyed living in the same town as him because you get to see your little sister."

"Of course I like seeing my *stepsister*. Janet is an innocent six-year-old who has nothing to do with the rift between me and my father."

"Well then, are you going to call him back?

"My father kills my mother and then marries his new wife a year later? I have very little to say to him. I only pay his bills because he had a biological hand in bringing me into the world. I owe him at least that respect, but other than that, I don't owe him anything–not even a phone call. If I want to see Janet, I can just call her mother."

Bryan can sense from my tone that I'm sick of this conversation. I'm not interested in anyone's opinion on what kind of relationship I "should" have with Keith Caraway, and I never have been.

"Got it."

I feel a slight twinge of guilt now. All this talk about my stepsister is making me think I owe her a FaceTime call. She really is innocent in all of this, and for whatever reason has formed an attachment to me. There are posters of me on her bedroom wall, for God's sake. I've got to do better.

"Do you have anything else on your schedule today that I don't have noted?" He asks.

"There's a woman," I tell him as he finishes tossing the ingredients into the blender.

"There's always a woman," he responds dismissively.

"This one is different."

"How?" He sounds unconvinced.

"She's infiltrated my dreams."

"Ooh, that is different."

He turns on the roaring motor of the blender as I watch the ingredients turn into a putrid brown color.

"She doesn't know who I am."

He quickly clicks the blender off.

"What do you mean she doesn't know who you are?"

"She doesn't watch football."

"Impossible."

"Not everyone watches sports, Bryan." I laugh.

"I know that. I'm saying it's impossible that she doesn't who you are. You've been on talk shows and gossip feeds for the last few years. You endorse four different products on television and have a half naked billboard in Times Square. Unless she's been living under a rock, there's no way she doesn't know who you are. She's hustling you."

"She's not." I say with great surety. "I told you, man, she's different."

"She's gotta be working you."

"You're so suspicious, young Padawan."

"My dad is an IRS investigator. He says everyone lies."

"I'm the liar in this situation."

"What did you tell her you did for a living? Did she even ask, because if she didn't ask, then she definitely knows who you are."

"Oh, she asked, but I evaded the question like I do defense when I'm in the pocket."

"So you lied."

"Evaded."

"If you like her so much, then why not tell her who you are? She'll probably be thrilled."

"I am an amazing human being–"

"Oh, brother."

"But she's going through some things right now, and I don't want to saddle her with my shit. The moment I tell her who I am will make her fair game for public scrutiny. I don't want that for her."

"Damn, you do like her."

He pours my smoothie in a tall glass and hands it to me. "Drink."

"Yeah, man, I think I might like her."

"Like her as in she might see the inside of this house one day?"

I never bring anyone to my apartment. It is my number one rule when sleeping with women. The moment you bring them inside your inner sanctum, the woman is already planning what dresser drawer she'll use for her sleepover underwear.

"Possibly."

"Then you better tell her and let her decide if she still wants to be bothered with you. I may not have a girlfriend, but it doesn't take an expert to know that she will not appreciate finding something like that out by anyone else but you."

I hate it when he's right.

"I'll take it under advisement."

I pop some of my pain meds, drink my new smoothie, which lo-and-behold tastes just like the other one, and then I head to the practice field.

I haven't seen my teammates since the game last week, and maybe a little time around them will help me get my mind off of the cute little doctor with the bewitching brown eyes.

SEVENTEEN

JETT

THE ENERGY of the locker room is focused but hushed when I walk in for the first time since my injury. Each member of the team is preparing for an intense day of practice in their own unique way. While we didn't win our last game, the good news is that we're actually still in the running to win our division because two other teams lost last week.

A few of the players give me a head nod or actually open their mouths to say hello as I make my way over to the physical therapy room. I wasn't expecting a ticker tape parade, but damn, they could be a little friendlier.

I don't want to be here as much as they don't want me here, but it's part of the job. While I won't get to play for most of the season, it's still my duty to get recommended therapies for my injury and cheer my teammates (and I use that word lightly) on to victory.

As much as I hate to admit it, Rivera, who is my

direct competitor on the team, is the only one who seems genuinely happy to see that I'm alive and breathing.

"How's the shoulder, Jett-Ski?" A nickname that some players call me in the league.

"Hurts like hell."

"That was a bad hit, man. He clearly crossed the line. They need to fine his ass for that."

"You and I both know they're not going to do that."

"If you were MVP of the league like Brady, they probably would."

"Well, them's the breaks. The MVP is beloved by the entire league and I'm... well, you know what I am."

"You're the future of this league. Don't forget it."

I can tell that Rivera has something more he wants to say because he's blowing smoke up my ass. I'm just not sure what it could possibly be.

"Jett, I need a favor from you, man."

Here it comes.

"You need a favor from me? What is it?"

"It's really a favor for my wife."

"I can't say no to Carla. Just tell me what it is and I'll do my best."

"She needs you to go out on a date with a woman."

"A friend of hers?"

"No."

"Someone terminally ill?"

"No, it's not like a last wish type of thing. It's a favor for a friend. She owns a matchmaking agency and asked Carla if we knew any players that would be willing to go on a date or two."

For a split moment, Adrienne's face pops into my

head. If I were to go on any sort of a real date, I'd rather it be with her.

"Rivera, I don't think–"

"I know it's a big ask, but Carla never asks me to use my celebrity for anything. The woman who owns the agency gave a big contribution to the Alliance last year, so I couldn't say no."

"But why me? Coach T wants me to lie low while I'm injured. I can't be videotaped or anything like that."

"You wouldn't have to do any pictures or video. The dates are all private, and we agreed they can be at places of your choosing for the sake of privacy. The owner wants to be able to say that her client roster includes prominent NFL players and actually not be lying on the advertisement copy."

"But I wouldn't be a client."

Women who go to matchmakers want what they paid for... a damn match. I am somebody's one-night stand, not a happily ever after. And did he say dates as in plural?

"On paper you would be."

"She couldn't use my name."

"She wouldn't, not without your consent."

"What do the women look like?"

Rivera laughs. "It's just a night or two out of your life. Show the woman a good time and you're done. Does it matter what she looks like?"

"And what if she falls madly in love with me?"

He laughs again.

"She won't. These women are smart."

"Ha! Fuck you."

"Is that a yes?"

"I assume sex is off the table."

"Yeah, there's a clause in the agreement about no sexual relations. I guess it interferes when trying to make a serious match."

"Then what's in it for me since I clearly won't be getting any ass?"

"They will interview me after the next game since I'm starting."

"Thanks for reminding me, so?"

"I'll be sure to mention you at least twice in the interview after we win," he says confidently. "We miss Jett's leadership, blah, blah, blah. Something like that."

"So you'll lie."

"Call it whatever you want. I prefer to describe it as continuing to keep your name in the hearts and minds of the people of New York City. "

"Why does everyone like you so much?" I (sort of) kid. "You're so full of it."

"Yeah, my wife tells me that all the time. So will you do it?"

I hesitate to answer.

"This is a big ask."

"For Carla?"

Rivera's wife is the head of the Nighthawk Wives Alliance. They hold a lot of fundraisers for local charities and when a new player joins the team; they send them a welcome basket. It's not just any basket either. The Alliance does their homework and researches favorite things of the player. My basket was full of Southwest Texas favorites, including homemade treats for Astro and a handwritten note.

I agree reluctantly.

"For Carla then."

He pats me gently on the back.

"Thank you, man. I know this was a big ask with everything that you've got going on."

"No problem."

I know I'm going to regret this.

"Let Carla know a restaurant you'd feel comfortable having dinner at. Depending on the place, she can make arrangements for total privacy. I'll tell her to be expecting your text. The date is Thursday."

"Agreed. Can I go now? I've got a dozen more specialist appointments for this cracked shoulder of mine today and you've just put me behind twenty minutes."

"You trying to get better and take my job again, Jett-Ski?"

This guy.

"No, man, I'm just trying to get mine back."

EIGHTEEN

ADRIENNE

I STARE at myself in the glass pane of the restaurant and wonder who is the woman staring back at me. I'm wearing a new blood red wrap dress that clings to my curves, conceals my pouch, and showcases just the right amount of cleavage. I spent way too much money on it, but it accentuates all my attributes and hides most of the flaws. I paired it with favorite black leather boots and a simple YSL clutch to dress it down because while I wanted to look good, I also didn't want to look as if I was trying too hard.

I'm going on a blind date with a man who has probably paid handsomely to meet the woman of his dreams. I feel like a fraud. I'm not the least bit interested in dating someone new, but every moment I spend doing something that I wouldn't have normally done when I was with Troy is a win for me. It feels like a victory.

I'll admit I was a little apprehensive about going

through with this evening. It all seems very unnatural. All I know is that I'm meeting someone named John, and he picked the place for the first date. I get to pick the place for the second date if there even will be a second one. We're meeting at some place called Piccolo Fiume, a restaurant I never heard of. It's a small Italian eatery tucked away on a narrow street in the heart of the meatpacking district. They don't even have a website. The only thing that makes me feel a little better about it is that Caroline promised that she has an entire file on John down to his underwear brand and that I'll be completely safe.

I take a deep breath to settle my nerves and open the door. As soon as I walk into the restaurant I am assaulted with the aroma of fresh garlic, capers and oregano. It smells delicious and immediately I'm assured that if nothing else, I'm going to get a good meal out of this.

I'm greeted by a jovial man with a head full of beautiful silver hair and olive skin.

"Welcome to Piccolo Fiume. Do you have a reservation?"

The restaurant is full. There are patrons seated at every table, and not one of them is occupied by a single man. Did he even show up?

"I'm meeting someone."

"Are you meeting a gentleman named John?"

"I am."

"Right this way, Signorina."

We walk alongside a painted mural of what I assume is an Italian landscape until we reach a narrow staircase.

"Watch your step."

As we climb the staircase, I grow even more nervous, so I begin to ramble.

"The food smells so delicious here. Are there any specialties you think I should try?"

"We make the best veal in the city. The veal piccata is my great-grandmother's recipe from the old country."

"You're the owner?"

"Yes, Signorina, for thirty years."

"You've been here for thirty years?"

"We've been in business a total of thirty and we've been at this location for fifteen of them."

Wow, my city never ceases to surprise me.

"I hope you enjoy your meal, Signorina. We pride ourselves on the freshness of our food and our service. Here's your table." The owner grins as he nods at me and turns to leave. "Your server will be with you shortly."

My date is waiting at the table, and the moment we lock eyes, my stomach drops.

This is not someone named Johnathan.

It's Jason.

Jason from The Wild Boar.

And he looks like he just had a million-dollar makeover.

He's dressed casually in a pair of dark jeans, a crisp white shirt, and a modern black leather jacket on top that looks like it cost more than everything I have on. The hair on his head is shorn low, but the beard on his face has grown somewhat in a week's time.

He looks panty-dropping hot.

"This has to be fate," he says with a grin so wide I

can't help but smile back. I think he's just as surprised to see me too.

I place my clutch on the table, take a seat and scan the room to get my bearings. We're seated in a small upstairs area that has four round top tables and chairs, but we're the only ones here. It's just us and the bartender.

"I thought your name was Jason."

"It is."

"I was told I was meeting someone named John."

"Are you disappointed?" He gnaws on a part of his bottom lip as he waits for my answer.

"No, just surprised."

"You look amazing, Adrienne. I'm a very lucky man tonight."

I blush for a moment and then compose myself.

"Forgive me for saying this, but you don't seem the type to use a matchmaking agency."

"Because of my extremely good looks?" He grins playfully.

"That and because you don't strike me as someone looking for a serious attachment."

"So you *do* think I'm good looking?"

I can't help but laugh at his high-spirited arrogance.

"Do you need me to say it, pretty boy?" I play along.

"Yes," he stares at me straight on. "I need you to say it."

"You look very... good tonight as well."

"Thank you. I agree. Now that we've gotten the pleasantries out of the way, why don't we look at the menu."

"The owner recommended the veal."

"Ooh, which dish?"

"The piccata."

"Let's get that and the marsala and share."

"Umm, ok."

"Red or white?"

I see he's back to playing his favorite game of this or that.

"Red."

"Perfect."

He raises two fingers at the bartender, who soon brings over a bottle of Cabernet Sauvignon for us.

"How did he know that two fingers meant red?"

"Two fingers meant Cabernet and I told him ahead of time."

"That's so weird."

"It's a football thing. We use hand signals and calls for everything."

"We?"

"I meant it's a guy thing. You know how men integrate a lot of things from sports into their lives. We're big kids like that."

"Actually, I don't know."

"The ex wasn't a big sports fan?"

"He watched sports news to kind of keep current, but he didn't really watch any games. He'd rather watch political or financial shows."

"Speaking of him, did you get your locks changed?"

"Turns out I was worried for nothing. He hasn't returned. I don't think it's an issue."

"Funny how we always end up talking about him."

"You brought him up," I reply defensively.

Our server for the evening approaches the table and asks us for our meal selections. We put in our orders and spend the next ten minutes talking about safe topics like the price of orange juice and how our pets are doing. Then he hits me with another round of questions.

"Apple or PC?"

"Can we answer without having to drink this time?"

"The rules call for drinking, but I'll give you an exception now that I know you can't handle your alcohol."

His cell phone buzzes several times and he checks it once but then turns it face down on the table.

"If you don't want to answer the question, then you drink otherwise you don't have to."

"And I get to ask you questions too, right?"

"Whatever you want. So the question was Apple or PC?"

"Apple of course."

"Me too," he grins. "Your turn."

"Jason or John?"

"Trust issues, maybe? I promise you my name is Jason. The agency came up with the whole alias thing for privacy. I thought I was meeting a woman named Trina."

He takes a small sip of his wine, swallows it slowly, then goes next.

"Top or bottom?"

"What do you mean?" I ask nervously, knowing exactly what he means.

"Do you like to ride on top or luxuriate on the bottom?"

A sudden warmth flushes the sides of my face and the back of my neck.

"That's a personal question."

"That's how the game is played."

"I don't want to answer it."

I could lie, but somehow I think this man could see right through it. I've never ridden on top and I don't want to admit to it.

"No problem, then drink." His eyes sparkle.

I look at my glass of wine and pause. It's not that I don't want to drink my wine, it's that I don't like the feeling of having to because I'm too afraid to answer a simple question. I'm not in high school anymore. I'm a grown ass woman and a doctor for goodness sake. Why do I fear his judgment? Why do I even care?

"Top," I lie without even flinching.

"Yeah," he says, shifting in his seat. "I can totally see that shit."

ADRIENNE

I HAD no idea that they made so many things in the color blush pink. There are forks, knives, plates, tablecloths, balloons, streamers, gift bags, candy dishes, serving platters, dresses, pants, blouses, hair accessories, shoes, and cake icing.

Every single damn thing in this banquet hall is in the color blush pink except for me. I'm dressed in a sky blue blouse with a pair of dark wash jeans and nude pumps. I forgot all about the theme.

The room is full of every woman in my family, and there are a lot of us. I work the perimeter of the room and greet each one, starting from my eldest great aunt (she's 93-years-old) to the youngest girl, my cousin Kira's daughter. When I'm finished all of my greetings, my mother gently pulls me to the side.

"Can I speak to you?"

I nod in acceptance and we step out of the hall and

into a side room which they sometimes use for coat overflow. I know because our family uses this hall for every major event we've ever had.

"You're wearing blue."

"I forgot about the pink."

"It was the one thing she asked for."

"I'm studying for boards, mom. I forgot."

"You're going to stick out in the pictures."

"Then I won't take any of the photos."

"Don't be ridiculous, that would break Cecily's heart."

Little does she know that I don't think it would.

"What do you want me to do, mom? I own nothing blush pink."

"I would have taken you shopping."

"Mom."

"Is this about Troy?"

"What?"

"Lorraine and Cecily mentioned something about Troy's Facebook page."

Those busy bodies.

"What about it?" I feign ignorance.

"Something is going on with you and Troy. Just tell me what happened because clearly it has you distracted."

"Mom, this is not the time. This is Cecily's day."

"But you're my daughter and I want to know that you're okay."

"I'm fine, mom." I sigh in defeat. "It was just an awful fight."

This is not the place to get into the details.

"And you're sure you're all right? What's with all the it's complicated mess."

"We had an argument, and perhaps the outcome felt a little complicated for him. For me, it's a little clearer. We're at different places in our lives."

My mom grabs my hand and holds it gently in her palm.

"Adrienne, did I ever tell you that your dad I had a huge argument before we were married? We broke up for twenty-three days."

I hear music playing. They're playing bridal shower games. I don't want to talk about this.

"Mom, we're missing all the fun."

She doesn't care.

"I consider my marriage and what happened within the confines of it sacred, but I'm telling you this so that you understand challenges are a part of any relationship worth its salt."

"I hear what you're saying but with all the respect in the world to you, Aunt Lorraine and Cecily, my relationship and how I choose to handle it is my business. I'm telling you I'm okay, that I forgot the damn wedding shower theme was blush pink, and that I don't want to talk about it anymore."

My mother's eyes widen at my tone and language. Out of respect for my elders, I never use foul language around them and certainly not at them, but she's like a dog with a bone when it comes to my happiness and I slipped up. It's infuriating that for some reason she thinks Troy is the only thing that can make me happy. Maybe it's because she only saw what I thought I saw, neither of us realizing that it was all a facade and my Mr. Perfect was just a mirage.

"You're upset."

"I'm sorry, mom. I shouldn't talk that way to you."

My mom's twin, Aunt Lorraine, dips her head into the room.

"Would you two come on? You're missing all the good door prizes. One of them is a Coach bag!"

"We're coming right now, Lo."

After she leaves, my mom says one more thing.

"Adrienne, I'm so proud of you and your accomplishments. You've done everything you've ever set your mind to, but don't let your ambition impede what really matters. At the end of this life, all you have left are the people who will carry on your legacy. You are my legacy. I know that your father and I will never be forgotten because of you. Family is what matters, whoever you decide to build it with."

A group of my cousins are wrapping Cecily in toilet paper and a group of her sorority sisters are wrapping a woman I don't know the same way. If I ever end up getting married, I promise I won't require any of my guests to take part in these asinine games. It's always been this way between Cecily and I, though. She loved the cartoons I thought were stupid. I loved books she thought were boring. We are polar opposites.

To pass the time, I get up and go to the buffet table to make a plate. I start off adding a few cucumbers, carrot sticks and a yogurt-based dipping sauce but then deviate from the "healthy" selections and into the more decadent options of fried chicken wings and Swedish meatballs.

Meat.

I crave it now.

I spear a meatball with one of Cecily's custom ordered blush pink colored toothpicks and devour it with gusto.

Welcome to my tummy, dear friends. It's been a long time.

Something about the consistency of the meat and the sauce remind me of the veal piccata I had on my date with Jason and it brings a smile not only to my face but to my entire body. I can't get that man out of my mind. He's both fantastic and frustrating all at the same time.

He's a flirt by nature, so I know that most of the things that he says to me are just a part of his playboy schtick. That's the frustrating part. But he makes me laugh and for a moment in time makes me forget about all the drama of the last few weeks. That's the fantastic part.

We discussed over homemade cannolis and freshly brewed espresso how we were both cleverly roped into our dates but decided that since it was ultimately to help out our mutual friends that we'd go on a second date per agency rules, of course. We also agreed to exchange cell phone numbers only in case of a last-minute cancellation or something like that, but as I get to know Jason better, I realize he isn't much of a rule follower.

More like a rule bender.

Jason: Christmas or New Year's Eve?

I get a random text out of nowhere and my heart hammers.

It's him.

Me: New Year's Eve

Jason: Me too!

Me: How can we always have the same answers? Lol!

Jason: Good friends often have a lot in common. I'm not surprised.

Friends.

My heart settles down.

Me: How's your shoulder?

Jason: That's why I'm texting.

Me: Oh?

Jason: I'm going to need surgery. I'm going to have to push the second date back.

My heart plummets.

Me: Just let me know when it will work for you and good luck.

There's a long pause between my last text and his eventual response.

I eat three more meatballs as I wait.

Jason: Thanks.

TWENTY

Three Weeks Later
ADRIENNE

ONE OF MY favorite things about this time of year is the fall foliage in Central Park. My father and I used to make a point of walking one of the park trails every year just to enjoy it. The leaves turn beautiful shades of red, orange and yellow and remind me that time is the one constant in this life. For some, it's moving at warp speed and they want to slow it down as much as possible. For others, it's moving at a snail's pace.

Right now, life is in snail mode. I haven't heard a peep from Jason and it's bringing all kinds of crazy out of me. It's not the same type of crazy I felt when I was stalking Troy's social media accounts. Rage fueled that crazy. This is something different.

I think I miss him a bit.

"Dr. Hodges, your last patient didn't show up," Penny announces.

"How long has it been?"

"Forty-five minutes and no phone call. I don't think they're showing up. I called them but got voicemail."

"Who was it?"

"The Kazinkski family."

"I don't think I know them."

"The kids are Dr. Hung's old patients. We transferred them to you when he left."

I check the time.

"Who's still here?"

"It's Thursday, so it's Dr. Osbourne's late day. She has patients for another hour."

"Ok, I'm going to finish up a file and then head out."

"Doing anything fun?"

"Going home to study with some friends and eat a chicken pot pie."

"That doesn't sound fun at all."

"That's the story of my life, Penny."

I'm part of a group of medical residents who are studying for the state boards in our respective specialities. Sometimes we meet virtually and other times we meet at each other's apartments. Tonight they're coming over to my place. I never had the group over before because Troy was usually here and he was the type that needed my attention when we were in the house together. I suppose now that I look back, that was another sign. He needed my undivided attention when we were together, and I wasn't capable of giving him that. I don't think anyone with a life of her own is.

Once I arrive home, I scratch Mitten's chin, disrobe, and throw on my favorite sweats. The gang will be here in an hour, so I have little time to warm up some cheap frozen appetizers. I toss a couple boxes of egg rolls in the oven and go through my mail. There's a letter in the pile without a stamp addressed to me. It's Troy's handwriting.

He's been in the apartment.

Fuck.

I look around to see if anything is out of place. Has he been inside here before? Maybe I should call the landlord in the morning and change the locks like Jason suggested.

Dear Adrienne,

I have spent our time apart reflecting on our relationship and my behavior. We have some issues, but I don't think they are impossible for us to overcome. I made a mistake. A big one. But I know you are not the type of person to write someone completely off because of one mistake. If you are ready to talk things through, then I'd love it if you would call me. I'm so sorry, Adrienne, and please know that I still love you. I hope you love me too.

Regards,

Troy

There is also another piece of paper inside the envelope. It's a trifold brochure of a banquet hall that he once mentioned in passing that he wanted us to consider for our wedding reception. This is insanity. He can't possibly think that there is any chance in hell that I'm marrying him. I put the letter and brochure back in the envelope and stuff it in my junk drawer in the kitchen. I'll deal with this later. Right now I have to get in study mode.

My study pals Owen, Paige and Keisha and I are seated cross-legged on my living room floor with our students materials spread out across the floor when the doorbell rings and my anxiety ratchets up a notch. After the letter I just read, I'm not sure what kinds of shenanigans Troy could be up to. Would he just pop by like this, wanting to talk things through?

"Is someone else coming over?" Owen asks with a concerned look on his face.

"No, I don't know who it is."

Owen is kind of the patriarch of the group and keeps us on point. We've been friends ever since medical school, and he's kind of like a big brother to me. He monitors me as I answer the door, which makes me feel a little less nervous.

I look through the peephole and notice there's a delivery man holding an enormous bouquet of flowers in his hands.

"Who is it?" Owen asks.

"Flowers," I say.

I answer the door and sign for the flowers.

"Hold on a second, y'all."

The group goes back to snacking on egg rolls as I read the card attached to the flowers, which reads: **Tacos or Steak?**

My entire body starts to tingle and a smile spreads across my face.

It's Jason.

He's okay.

"Those flowers are incredible," Paige says. "What are they, freesias? I can smell them from here."

"Are they from the asshat?" Owen asks harshly.

All three of my study buddies know that Troy and I

broke up and they know it was bad, they just don't know the details. I can't seem to tell anyone what happened. Outside of Dena, only Jason knows.

"No," I say as I try to restrain my giggles. "They're not."

I grab my cell phone off the counter so I can respond.

"One more second," I tell the group.

Me: Tacos

Jason: I know you like meat, so I wasn't sure.

Me: I take it you're okay?

Jason: Fantastic. Doctors took good care of me.

Me: What did you get done?

Jason: Pins and rods.

Me: Where'd you have it done?

Jason: Mercy West.

My hospital is one of the best in the area. I'm relieved he could get a decent surgical consultation and procedure.

Me: Thank you for the flowers. You didn't have to though.

They look expensive.

Jason: You're welcome.

Me: When do you want to have tacos?

Jason: Thursdays are our scheduled date night.

I look over at the gang and for the first time wish like hell that I could reschedule this study group. I'd rather see Jason any day of the week.

Me: I can't tonight.

There's a long pause before he responds.

Jason: Did you replace me with someone else from the agency?

I think he's playing with me. Sometimes it's hard to tell via text.

Me: No:)

Jason: Then why can't we have dinner TONIGHT?

Because I haven't heard from you in three weeks.

Because I can't just bail on all the important things in my life when you call.

Because I need to protect my heart from you.

Me: I'm studying with friends.

Jason: Next Thursday?

That's so far away, but I don't want to seem too eager and suggest something sooner.

Me: Cool.

I need to remember. We're just friends.

Jason: Cool:)

TWENTY-ONE

ADRIENNE

THIS HAS BEEN the longest week of my life. I don't think that I've ever looked more forward to a night out with a man as much as I do this one, and that's both thrilling and frightening for me. According to the agency's protocol, the second date was supposed to be my pick, but since he initiated asking me for tacos, I thought I'd just follow his lead.

By Monday night I wasn't sure if there was going to be a date at all, I hadn't heard from him, but I was adamant that it wouldn't be me who would reach out. I was already getting too invested. Too excited. I needed to pull back some. We were just friends who were sticking to a commitment we made. This is not an actual date.

On Wednesday night, I received another bouquet of flowers from Jason with a card that simply stated the address of the Mexican restaurant we will meet at.

. . .

Reservation is for: 7pm
2178 Wheeler Street
_-J_

"You sound excited, A." Dena notices.

"I don't know what you're talking about."

"You know exactly what I'm talking about. What are the chances that the man I set you up with is the same hottie from the bar? If that's not kismet, I don't know what is."

"Now you're taking credit for setting me up?"

"Absolutely, girl. You fought me tooth and nail about going on this date. If it wasn't for me, you probably would've never seen hot bar guy again."

"It's not a real date though, Dena. This is a favor for Caroline on both of our parts. Which I'm still wondering what kind of connection someone like him has to her."

"Someone like him?"

"I don't think a guy like him travels in Caroline's circles."

"Well, confidentiality is a huge part of Caroline's brand, so I have no idea. She won't even tell me his full legal name, and I didn't tell her you knew him from the bar. At this point, I'm staying out of it. So if you want more answers, you're just going to have to ask the man himself."

I already embarrassed myself once by acting surprised that he'd attended college, so I'm not trying to go there again. It's not as if all of Caroline's friends are wealthy. Dena isn't. It's really none of my business how he knows her. I'm going to leave it alone.

"So is everything completely over with Troy?"

"Totally, oh, did I mention I think he's been in my house again?"

"What do you mean? That sounds like a situation."

"I think he was grabbing the rest of his things when he knew I wouldn't be home, but he left me a letter."

"He's such a creeper."

"With a banquet hall brochure inside."

"Okay, now that's actually really creepy."

"I'm going to get the locks changed. That'll solve all of that."

I just have to remember to call the landlord when he'll actually be available to pick up the phone. He never listens to voice messages.

"Good idea. So when's the next date with hot bar guy? Where are ya'll going? It's ladies' choice this time isn't it?"

"That's confidential information."

"Ooh, you're such a little bitch!" she laughs hysterically.

"Sorry, not sorry. Bye, Dena."

Mexican restaurants are typically casual, so tonight I'm dressed in a pair of jeans with a purple fitted v-neck t-shirt, a swipe of violet shadow on my eyelids and a pair of white chucks. I throw on my Gucci crossbody bag to elevate the look and a short black puffer jacket. The jeans are tighter than I remember, probably because I've been eating everything under the sun since the break-up, so to eliminate any panty lines I decide to wear my jeans sans underwear.

Jason has picked yet another out-of-the-way restaurant with impeccable service and delicious authentic food. A small Mariachi band plays once I enter inside and they follow behind us as we sit at our table in a private section of the restaurant. Jason loves the music and waves his hand to the melody as each member plays their trumpet, guitar and violin.

It's clear that his surgery was successful, and he's in less pain than he was before. He looks lighter both on his feet and in spirit. That makes my heart happy, but only because I'm a doctor, of course. Not for any other reason.

"Hey, beautiful," he says as he leans in to give me a one-armed hug.

Jason towers over me by well over a foot, so when he pulls me in for an embrace, my face meets him mid-chest. It's a great place for my face to be. He smells like a heady mixture of soap, leather and cinnamon. I reluctantly pull from the embrace first. If I hadn't, I would have settled into his chest like Mittens when she wants to snuggle with me. That's how broad and luscious his chest feels. Like a high-end hotel bed.

"Did you like your grand entrance?"

"It was something all right."

"They're going to come back and play for us once our food comes to the table."

"Really?"

"Yeah, that's part of the ambiance here."

"I wonder where the other patrons are?"

"I heard this place is way busier on the weekend."

"Sure, that makes sense. I can tell that your shoulder is better."

"I can't put any weight on it and have limited range of motion, but the swelling has gone down significantly since the procedure."

"I'm glad."

He stares at me with a goofy grin on his face. "I am too."

"So, does this place have black bean tacos?" I ask, joking around.

"Hell no, and if that's what you want to order, this date is already over."

"I think you have a prejudice against vegetarians. We're good people."

"Not my kind of people."

"So you don't trust people who don't like animals *and* who don't eat meat? That seems like an oxymoron."

"Call it whatever you want to call it. I am who I am."

"Said Sam I am."

His eyes light up.

"Your favorite childhood book too?"

"One of them," I admit. "I can see the tattered orange hardback cover in my head. My mom used to read it to me all the time."

"Mine too. This friendship of ours is really starting to have some legs."

"Yeah, I guess so."

Jason orders a variety of tacos and sides for the table

because according to him, there's just no way you can choose just one kind.

He was right.

The food is to die for.

After fifteen minutes of steak taco heavenly silence and more Mariachi music we chat again.

"Guac or sour cream?" he asks.

"Guacamole, obviously." I point to my disappearing blob of homemade guacamole. "What about you?"

His portions look pretty even.

"I like them both, but if I had to choose, it would be sour cream."

"Oh, so we finally have a different answer."

He stares into my eyes as he takes a bite and chews sexily slow, if that's even a thing.

"Yeah, we have some differences, but only in the best ways."

His eyes drop to my breasts and immediately I can feel my nipples pucker inside the cups of my bra.

"Are you sure you don't want anything to drink?" he asks.

"I have work tomorrow." I place my taco down. "You know I'm starting to feel like you spend most of our time together trying to get me drunk."

"Is that how it seems?"

"A little, yeah."

"I apologize if that's how it comes off. It's just that sometimes it seems as if you have the weight of the world on your shoulders. The alcohol loosens you up."

"So you're saying I'm uptight?"

"No, ma'm, not at all. When I first saw you dancing at

the jukebox without a care in the world, I knew you weren't uptight. It wasn't until you remembered that there were other people in the room that you tensed up."

"Am I boring without a drink?"

"You're taking what I'm saying the wrong way, darlin'. There's nothing boring about you at all. It's just that I don't know you well enough yet to know how to relieve some of the stress you're carrying around. But when I figure it out, I will be sure to replace any drink you might crave with whatever *it* is."

I crack a small smile and continue chewing my food while he continues to focus on me and only me.

"Look at me, Adrienne."

The sudden thick commanding bass of his voice sends a shudder down my spine and settles in between my legs. My eyes flick up instantly, as if I was powerless to do otherwise.

"I can think of another way to make you forget all about work and bad boyfriends."

A piece of soft taco settles in my throat.

"You do?"

"Would you be interested?

"Um, if you're talking about what I think you are that would be against the arrangement with the agency, wouldn't it?"

"Ah, the pesky no sex clause."

"Yeah, that one."

"I'm going to put in the suggestion box that she adjust agency regulations."

"I think the limits are there for a reason."

I take a long gulp of my ice water.

Suddenly my throat is dry.

Suddenly I imagine all the ways that a man like Jason could help me unwind.

Suddenly I can feel the seam of my jeans digging into the folds of my pussy and I'm getting damper by the minute.

Crap, I should have worn panties.

"You should see your face right now," he says, as if he's been completely kidding with me the last few minutes.

I feel so stupid.

"Yeah, you got me," I fake chuckle.

"Yeah, I definitely got you."

TWENTY-TWO

ADRIENNE

AFTER DINNER, Jason asks if I would mind walking for a bit before we end the date. Of course I don't mind. Any more time I get to spend with him is a bonus. He's a lot of fun to be around. Who wouldn't want to hang with him?

"Did you enjoy your meal?"

"You know I did," I say, rubbing my protruding tummy. I'm not even embarrassed about it. Not with him.

"That's a full tummy well earned," he mocks.

"You know, a lot of off-the-beaten-path restaurants. Are you a foodie?"

"I've never been to either of those places before. I just did my homework and heard they were good spots for authentic cuisine."

"You've never eaten at either place?"

"No, why?"

"They treated us like VIP customers. Both times we

basically had part of the restaurant to ourselves. I thought it was because you were a favorite customer."

"I think Thursdays are slow nights for both places. I was looking for a quieter type atmosphere."

"Privacy is important to you?"

"I just remembered what you said about my shoulder and crowds. I didn't want to risk bumping into anyone, especially with all this new hardware they put inside me keeping it together."

"That's good to know that you're actually listening to me." I grin.

"Oh, I'm definitely listening, darlin'."

We walk in silence for a few moments and I'm completely at ease. For once, I don't feel the need to fill the space with chatter. It's just me and Jason and a lot of staring eyes.

That's another thing.

I'm thinking he prefers smaller restaurants because he definitely garners a lot of attention from both men and women. It's the craziest thing, but I imagine they gawk because he's typically the tallest person in the room and usually the most handsome. It's difficult not to speculate what people may think when they see me walking down the street with him.

Are they together?

He's too good for her.

I know those aren't healthy thoughts, but I can't help it. If he and I had met years ago in high school, he is not someone I would have been friends with. That's just a reality. I didn't run in the popular circles of the beautiful people. I was the nerdy girl who spent most of her down time studying or watching old musicals with her mom.

"So last week you said you were studying?"

"Yes, with a few friends of mine at my house."

"They're all doctors?"

"Yes, we're studying for our boards. When I pass, I'll be a board certified pediatrician. It's just another credential to let clients know that I've received attentional training in my specialty."

"You said you were studying at your house?"

"Yes, that's right."

"All female doctors?"

"There's three of us and one guy– Owen."

"Owen?"

"He was the first person to show me the ropes when I got into medical school. I was younger than the average student, and he took a special interest in me. He's like a big brother."

"I bet."

I cock my head to the side unsure of what he's suggesting.

"He really is like a brother to me."

"Is he married?"

"No," I chuckle.

"Was he friends with the ex?"

"Absolutely not. They didn't really talk that much to each other. Just cordial greetings."

"Yep."

"Yep, what?"

"Big brother probably has a crush on you."

"You've never even met him," I scoff. "You don't know what you're talking about."

"If he's been hanging around you this long, I think I do."

"Men and women can have platonic relationships, Jason. Look at us. We have a lot of fun together and there's nothing romantic about it whatsoever."

His face scrunches up into a scowl

"We're different."

I shrug my shoulders

"I don't think so. Hey, can we stop in here?" I ask.

We stop at a local electronic store that's open for another hour. One perk about living in Manhattan is that many of the stores will stay open longer than you see in other cities simply because there are more people out still shopping.

"What are we looking for?"

"I'm thinking about getting a new television."

"That's right up my alley. What kind are we looking for?" he asks excitedly.

"Something small. I just need one in the bedroom."

"Do you have one in there right now? Is it broken?"

"No, um."

"Don't tell me. The ex had something against television."

"In the bedroom he did. He needed a perfectly quiet room devoid of extraneous sound or light."

"Or laughter."

I turn my lips up in a sardonic smile.

"You saw my relationship at its lowest point. There were some good times."

"You should set a higher bar."

"Oh, really... and when's the last time you were even in something that remotely looked like a relationship?"

"I think I'm offended."

He grabs his chest playfully as if he's clutching his pearls.

"I think you and I can both agree that you are not offended by the slightest. You don't seem the type."

"Ok, you got me. I'm not a relationship type of dude but there're reasons for that."

"Which are?"

"I don't want to disappoint someone that I love."

"That might be inevitable."

"Not the way I do it."

"And what magical way is that?"

"I'm honest."

"Please explain."

"I spend time with women who understand that our relationship will be a physically satisfying connection and nothing more."

"And they go for that?"

"I have had no complaints yet."

"I could never do that."

"Why not? We both get something out of it and there are no unmet expectations. No hurt feelings."

"I doubt that," I mutter under my breath.

"What's that, beautiful?"

"I said what about this one?

"Twenty-seven inches is a respectable size. Not obnoxiously big. Where would you put it? On a wall or a tv table?"

"Probably just on top of my dresser. I don't want to spend the extra funds to have it mounted on a wall."

"This thirty-two inch is on sale. How about this one? I know someone who can mount it for you at a discount."

"Really?"

"Yeah, get it."

It takes ten minutes to find someone who isn't busy to help us. I honestly was ready to leave, but Jason seems more excited about the tv than I am. He wants me to get it. So we wait. While the sales associate goes in the back to find us the model on sale because there are no more on the showroom floor, Jason watches a news program on one of the model televisions and becomes unusually quiet.

I tap him on the back of his good shoulder.

"Hey, you all right?"

"Yeah, I'm good."

"What's this show?"

"It's a sports newscast."

"The Rangers again?"

"Not this time. They're talking about football."

"Oh."

The program repeatedly shows a highlight where a player was hit pretty hard.

"Ugh," I comment. "Football is so brutal. I don't know how you watch it. Look at how hard they hit that guy. He's probably still seeing stars."

"Have you ever watched a football game from start to finish, Adrienne?"

"Nope."

He seems displeased with my answer and I wonder if

in someway I've offended him yet again. I seem to have a knack for that. I guess he's a touchy guy.

"I mean, it's just that I've taken an oath to care for human beings and save lives," I explain. "To put your health on the line like that, every game seems self destructive to me. I know you enjoy watching it, but think about the men that are playing it. You've got to ask yourself why the put themselves in harms way like that."

"Because it's fun?"

"I think the more accurate word is dangerous."

"It's a highly strategic sport."

"Yeah, like war."

An irritated look covers Jason's face.

"Where's your tv?" he asks impatiently.

"He's ringing it up. Crap, I didn't even think about how I'm going to get this thing home. Let me ask him how much delivery is."

"Uh-uh, we're going to take this baby to your house and set it up so you and Mittens can watch Patrick Swayze and Baby all comfy in your bed if you want."

"But your shoulder."

"We'll figure it out."

And figure it out we do.

TWENTY-THREE

ADRIENNE

A STAFF ASSOCIATE carries the box outside, and another one waits with us as we call for an Uber. The driver has a completely empty trunk, and the tv fits perfectly inside. Due to traffic, we take about twenty minutes to get to my apartment and once we arrive, Jason slips the driver an extra twenty dollar bill to help him get the box in the elevator. We figure we can both slide it out together once we get to my floor.

"This is it," I tell him.

I fiddle inside my bag for my key and unlock the door. The lights are on in every room and I second guess if in my excitement for the date I forgot to turn off my lights. That question is quickly answered when the toilet flushes and my ex-fiancé exits the bathroom.

What the hell?

The two of us stand stock still, staring at each other, but I can feel a stormy energy rolling off of Jason. Immediately,

I feel the need to explain. This doesn't look good. Even though I don't owe Jason any explanation at all. We're just hanging. I have to keep reminding myself of that.

We're just two friends hanging.

"What are you doing inside my house, Troy?"

"What is he doing here?" Troy retorts, pointing to Jason.

"Adrienne, where's the cat?"

I look nervously around for Mittens and notice that the office door is shut again.

"Did you lock up Mittens again?"

"How does he know you own a cat?" Troy says angrily. "Has he been in here before? Have you been cheating on me this whole time, Adrienne?"

Troy glares at Jason as if he's some sort of complicated puzzle he can't put together.

"He's a friend who has been invited inside and you are neither. Please leave."

Jason sighs heavily and then steps closer to Troy, overshadowing him with his height and sheer dominance. "You're having trouble with this breakup and that's understandable, man. Adrienne is a kick ass superstar, and you fucked up. But sometimes in life you've got to take the loss and move on. This is one of those times. The lady wants you to leave, and she wants you to leave your keys when you do."

"The lady can speak for herself," Troy rebuts.

"How many other ways can I say it to you, Troy?" I say. "We're over."

"Didn't you read my letter?"

"What letter?" Jason looks irked.

"Do you answer to him now, Adrienne!"

This is the first time I'm noticing that Troy's eyes look unbalanced. I'm not sure if it's from lack of sleep or something more chemical.

"Are you getting any sleep, Troy? Are you drunk or something?"

Jason turns his head and gives me an annoyed look.

"He's fine."

Troy moves towards me, but Jason lifts his good arm and stops him dead in his chest. I can feel the thump in my own.

"I can't sleep, honey." Troy explains. "I miss you so much. I knew you still loved me."

"She may have loved you once, but she's fucking me now, so I will not tell you again. Take your loopy ass somewhere else and get the hell out of my girl's apartment."

I'm floored by the words coming out of Jason's mouth, not only because they're total lies, but because a part of me wishes to God they weren't.

Troy moves forward another step to plead his case, and I step back. He's acting totally out of character and I've got to say I'm a little frightened. If Jason wasn't here, I'm not sure what would have happened. I'm not sure I would have been able to get him out on my own.

"Adrienne, please, I want us to work things out. I will do anything you ask me to. Just give me a chance to make it up to you. We can postpone the wedding, go to counseling, whatever you want."

"This is getting embarrassing, dude," Jason says mockingly to Troy.

"You need to make a choice once and for all, Adrienne. Me or this guy!"

"This sounds like the same lame threat you made at the bar," Jason says. "There is no choice to be made. I mean look at me and look at you."

"She doesn't even know you!"

Troy is becoming unhinged.

"I think you live on some sort of alternate universe where you can just sleep with whoever you want wherever you want and then question what I'm doing," I say.

"Did you ever stop to ask yourself why I cheated on you? Because being in a relationship with you was hell and—"

The truth finally rears its ugly head.

"You're drunk," Jason palms Troy's entire face with his hand. "Time for you to go."

"It was hell for me too!" I yell back. "Leave my keys on the kitchen counter and get out. I never want to see or hear from you again. If you trespass in my house again, I'll call the police."

After Jason releases his hand, Troy stares daggers at Jason. "I don't know who the hell you are or what you've done to her, but you can have her."

"Are you still yapping?" Jason pretends to yawn as if he's unfazed. "Do I need to throw you out myself?"

Troy reaches in his pocket and slams the key on the table and even has the nerve to kick my new television box on his way out.

After the door slams shut, I run to the office and look for Mittens. She's sitting on top of my desk, looking perfectly content. I pick her up and bring her out into the living room, holding her close.

"I can't believe I was going to marry that man."

"She okay?" Jason asks, referring to Mittens.

"She's perfect, but how's my new television?"

"I'm sure it's fine. That box is padded with so much styrofoam. Tiny Tim did nothing but make himself look stupid."

"Tiny Tim?"

"My nickname for your gross error in judgement."

I sit on my couch and kick off my shoes as I take a few cleansing breaths.

"That was kind of scary," I admit. "I've never seen him act so... angry."

"I would never let nothing happen to you, beautiful. He would've had to have broken my other shoulder to stop me. He's lucky, I was two-seconds away from body slamming his ass."

A feeling of relief overwhelms me, and I stand back up and grab Jason around the waist. Resting my chin on his chest.

"Thank you for dinner and thank you for tonight. You seem to keep coming to my rescue."

The silver flecks in his eyes make them shimmer and momentarily make my legs feel like a pair of soggy noodles. As if he can feel me dropping, he grabs me around the waist with his good arm and pulls me in tighter.

The look of yearning on his face is unexpected and dangerous.

It's the look of a man who could ask me anything right now, and I'd say yes.

Even if it means my destruction.

TWENTY-FOUR

ADRIENNE

SOMETHING in the air has shifted and there is an erotic quiet between us.

I can practically hear the blood rushing through my veins.

If he kisses me, I'll let him.

If he doesn't, I may just die.

His head bends lower as his hand slides slowly down to my ass and settles there. Then his mouth inches closer to mine, excruciatingly slow. Either Jason is playing around with my head or he takes great pleasure in torturing me because at this point I have an ache between my legs that only he can relieve.

When our lips finally connect, it doesn't feel like a normal kiss. It feels as if he is seducing me with his mouth. Worshiping it. Peppering kisses on the corners of my mouth and then thrusting his tongue deeper inside with purpose and ownership.

As he continues to make love to my mouth, his hand travels lower and in between my legs, right at the center seam of my jeans. He uses two of his fingers to push the seam into me and against my rapidly swelling clit. I moan from the pleasure radiating from my core and he growls with approval that I'm responding.

He releases my lips as we come up for air.

"Let's bend the rules," he says in a deep, thick voice, and I know exactly what he means.

"Okay," is my one word response.

I don't even recognize my own voice as it cracks with need and lust.

"Is this the way to your bedroom?"

I nod silently yes.

Jason grabs my hand and starts walking toward my bedroom, closing the door and leaving Mittens alone in the living area.

Sorry, Mittens, but I think tonight it's every kitty for herself.

I'm extremely nervous for a lot of reasons. I've had sex with three people in my life: The boy who took my virginity on prom night then never came back home from college, the guy I was dating before Troy (he accidentally fell in love with his best friend), and Troy.

Based on my experience with those three men, I am well aware that I'm not the best lover in bed. I'm just not. My partners didn't expect or require much from me but to lie down and receive, so that's what I know how to do. I'm a missionary position queen and not particularly great at that. At least I don't think I am.

I've never had an orgasm while having sex, only

when I've masturbated, so it has to be something I'm doing wrong. What if Jason expects me to be a good lover? What if he's disappointed by me? Maybe I should stop this before it goes any further.

"I can only imagine what you're thinking, Adrienne."

That maybe all of this is moving too fast after Troy. That I don't know what the hell I'm doing.

"But I want you to know that I see you and tonight you're going to see what I see."

I do not know what he's talking about, but I just go with it.

"Okay."

"Stand in front of the mirror."

There's a big mirror that tops my dresser. It's an old piece from my mom's house that I brought with me when I moved into my apartment.

Jason stands behind me and wraps his arm around me and into the waistband of my jeans.

"Look at yourself in the mirror."

It's harder to do than I thought. My eyes naturally veer down.

"Eyes up," he demands.

I look in the mirror and look at him. God, he's beautiful. Then I look at myself and wonder how I ended up with this man in my bedroom. It hasn't been long, but I feel like I've known him my entire life. He's practically a stranger, but I feel like I've shared more of myself with in the last few weeks than I ever have with anyone before.

"I see you," he says again as he expertly unbuttons

my jeans and slides down the zipper. "And I like everything about what I see."

I suck in a breath.

I'm scared.

"Eyes ahead," he demands again. "Pull off your shirt."

His hand rests right at my open waistband as I go to lift my shirt. As I lift higher, his hand slides lower.

"Now the bra."

As I reach behind my back and unhook my bra, his hand goes even lower and now several of his fingers are between my slick folds.

My eyes grow heavy with pleasure.

"Eyes open."

I pop them back open.

"I see you so clearly, Adrienne. I see a fucking goddess. A queen. I would love to paint you. Maybe you'll allow me the privilege one day. Now hold your tits for me. Hold them high and use your thumbs to play with your nipples. Pet them for me while I pet your pussy."

I whimper as Jason deftly plays in between my folds. Working his fingers on either side of my clit.

"Do you see what I see, beautiful?"

I can't talk.

Does he actually expect me to answer? I'm going to come in two more seconds.

"I see a woman who is about to come all over my hand and look exquisite when she does. I see a woman who's going to say the name of the man who owns this pussy tonight."

Yeah, I'm definitely about to see stars.

My knees buckle and I fall forward with my hands on the dresser.

"Eyes up."

My whimpers are turning feral.

I am going to come soon. It's tearing through me like a summer storm and it's going to be epic.

He leans forward with his mouth to my ear.

"Who's pussy is this tonight?"

I moan louder.

"Eyes in the fucking mirror, Adrienne. I'm not going to tell you again."

My head pops back up. His hand moves even faster now.

"Whose pussy does this belong to tonight?"

"Yours," I whisper.

"Whose?"

"Yours," I say louder.

Two of his fingers slip effortlessly inside of me and start pumping in and out.

"Tell me again, beautiful," he growls in my ear.

"Yours!"

"That's right, baby. This pussy is mine tonight."

My head has the sensation of exploding into tiny little iridescent pieces. The orgasm rocks my entire body and knocks me senseless. I am breathing heavily and barely holding on as I feel small aftershocks, and still he demands more.

"Eyes. Up."

I look up with dazed eyes and watch raptly as Jason sucks the taste of me off each of his fingers.

"Damn, you taste delicious."

All I can do is blush after what's just happened. I don't even know what to even say in response to that.

"I need you to strip now. I need a better taste."

I slowly peel off my jeans and a sinister look crosses Jason's face once he notices that I've gone commando. He sits on the edge of the bed and I hesitate, remembering what I saw Troy doing on this bed not that long ago. I don't know if I can have sex in my own bed right now. I don't know that I'll ever be able to again.

"I know what you're thinking, but this is why I brought you in here," he says. "I could have easily fucked you a million other places in this apartment, but it has to be here and you know why."

"Actually, I don't know why."

"It has to be here so that we can obliterate him from your consciousness just like you wanted the night I met you. When you sleep in this bed from now on, all you're going to remember is how I made you scream my name."

Oh, my fucking god.

"Now strip."

TWENTY-FIVE

ADRIENNE

I FINISH STEPPING out of my jeans and stand completely naked before him, totally nervous.

"You're gorgeous, Adrienne. Damn, I'm lucky. Now, for obvious reasons, you're going to have to help me get my clothes off, okay?"

"Yes."

"Good, let's start with the shirt since that will be the hardest."

I obviously know how to take off a person's clothing when they're injured. I'm a doctor. But Jason likes to control things, almost in the way a conductor leads an orchestra through a beautiful symphony.

I carefully help slide his arm out of the sling and out of his t-shirt. Then we put his arm back in the sling. This is the first time I notice the ink on his back. It's unique and so sexy. It's a colorful landscape with a plane taking flight. There must be some sort of meaning behind it. It looks like it took days to complete.

"Now the jeans."

Undressing someone before sex is a very intimate act that I've only seen in movies. It's not something I've ever done before, but it's not as uncomfortable as I thought it would make me feel. It's actually very sexy. I unfasten Jason's jeans to reveal a pair of black boxer briefs covering a large bulge inside.

Jason sits in the middle of the bed against the headboard and taps his thigh.

"Come sit on your knees in front of my face."

"What?"

"You heard me. Front and center."

I close my eyes, embarrassed at the position I'm in but needy just the same. He speaks to me with his face dangerously close to my core and his hand stroking my thigh.

"We're still good, right Adrienne? Because I can stop at any point if you're uncomfortable."

Stop? Hell, no.

"Uh-uh, I'm good."

"That's excellent to hear because I'm about to taste you again, which means you're going to come again. And when you do this time, remember to say the name of the man giving you all this pleasure. You understand?"

"Yes."

"Good girl."

He grabs one of my ass cheeks with his hand and pulls me close to his face. He starts slowly by licking just the tip of my clit with his tongue and it drives just about bad-shit crazy. It's like my body has a mind of its own as I grind myself into his face.

He loves my reaction and starts chuckling. The rumble of his laughter vibrates against my core and makes me needier than I already was. He lightly pats my ass cheeks with alternating slaps as he continues to lick my pussy.

My moans turn almost to sobs and I slide my hands around head, wanting him to dive even deeper inside me if that's possible. He's eating me out more aggressively now. Sucking and pulling at my clit and smacking my butt so hard that I bet the neighbors can even hear me.

It feels exquisite.

It feels life changing.

I am about to come and I barely can catch my breath.

"Don't stop," I beg softly.

I'm getting so close.

"Whose pussy is this tonight?" he demands to know again.

"Yours."

"And who am I?"

"Jason."

"That's right. Say my name again."

"Jason!"

He flutters his tongue against my pussy rapidly, then pulls his head back just in time to watch me fall apart. My heart is racing, and my breaths are heavy, but then they almost stop as I notice that he's pulled his penis out of his boxers and his stroking himself.

"You are so beautiful when you come, Adrienne.

That shit turns me on. I could watch you come all day, every day."

Jason likes to watch. That turns me on too.

"I know you said you like to be on top, so why don't you hop on and ride me, baby. I can't wait to get inside of you. Damn, I'm so excited I almost forgot. There's a condom in the back pocket of my jeans. Why don't you grab it? I'll wait right here."

He continues stroking himself as he watches me with a hunger in his eyes.

Shit, how am I going to finesse my way out of this one. I told him I prefer the top, but I've never done it before and his dick looks like the size of my baseball bat. I may not know much, but I know that it's going to be a tight fit. I rummage through his pockets and find three condoms and wonder if he always carries this many on him. Probably. This man probably has lots of sex.

I place two of them on my nightstand and hand him the other one.

"You want to do it or you want me to?" he asks.

"You."

He pauses for a moment. "You nervous, Adrienne?"

"A little."

"Don't think about him. Focus only on me and you."

He has no clue. My hesitance has nothing to do with Troy and everything to do with my amateur skills.

"Open the package for me."

I tear open the condom wrapper and hand it to him. With one good arm this man has made me come twice and now he's rolling a condom perfectly down his enormous dick like he's done this one-handed a million times.

"Come ride me Texas style."

I don't even know what that is, but I don't need to know because Jason guides me into position on top, back to him, facing the mirror again.

"If you're nervous about my size, take it slow. We've got all night and I guarantee you it will fit."

He rubs me gently between my legs as I position myself on top of him and slowly lower myself. I pray that this position doesn't split me wide open. He's so thick and I'm so tight that I'm not sure if it's going to work, but as I look at him massaging my clit in the mirror — I feel empowered. I feel like a fucking siren. A sex goddess. I feel like I can actually do this.

"Move slightly forward," he says through gritted teeth. "That's it. Now rock your hips back and forth a bit. Yes, fuck. You're halfway there. Give me some more of this sweet ass pussy. I need to be totally inside you."

"Jason." I beg for something, and I don't even know what. For more? For it to stop? I don't know.

"That's right, baby. Jason owns this pussy. It belongs to me. Now open it up wider so I can get inside."

I feel slicker and slicker with each word he utters, and I am moving further down until he is balls deep inside me. I have to stop moving for a moment and allow myself to adjust. The full feeling of him inside of me takes my breath away.

"Fuck, Adrienne. You feel so good."

I slowly work my hips up and down and rock them back and forth. I feel stuffed, but in the best way possible.

I look at his contorted face in the mirror behind me and feel totally powerful.

I am making him feel that way.

Me.

His hand releases my clit, and he pushes my back until I am resting my palms on the bed in front of him. He pulls my hips up and back and now he's in control. He is fucking me from the back and for a split second I see a flash of Troy and that woman in my mind and I tense up, but Jason can feel it and talks me through it.

"Look ahead at the mirror, Adrienne. Do you see me fucking you? Do you see me?"

"Yes."

"Do you see what you do to me?"

"Yes." My response is almost guttural because of how deep inside me he is.

"Yeah, I know you do. And you know what else, beautiful, you will not be able to walk tomorrow without remembering how good you made me feel today."

He rises on his knees now, slides his hand in the back of my hair and gently leans my head down on the bed. His penetrating strokes are deep and hard from this angle. I'm full to the brim, but yet I want more.

"More."

"What, baby?"

"I want more."

He pounds me with more punishing strokes that have me clawing at my comforter for dear life.

"Oh, shit!"

He's growling and grunting, about to come himself, and I think I'm going to come with him.

"Oh, Jason."

"Fuccckkk!"

We both explode and fall on our sides in exhaustion and bliss. After slowly coming down off my first vaginal orgasm, I make a confession.

"That was incredible."

"That was just the beginning, baby." He grins proudly. "This pussy belongs to me for the rest of the night.

JETT

I'M PROPPED on my right side and staring at the most beautiful woman I've ever met. One of her eyelids flutters and she smiles when she sleeps. I wonder if she knows that about herself, or would it be presumptuous of me to think that she's happily grinning because she had some of the best sex of her life last night? I know I definitely did.

I've had plenty of sex over the course of my adult years, but perhaps there's some truth about enjoying it more when you actually start to give a damn about the person you're doing it with. It's not to say that I didn't have respect for the women I've laid with. I did. But this was different.

This is different.

Adrienne's luscious body curves and bends like an exquisite sculpture. She truly is a work of art. I adjust myself onto my stomach so that I can use my free hand to trace the side of her body lightly with my fingertips.

Starting at her curls and slowly down her neck, to her shoulders, then her back until I pause at the curve of her spine. There's a slight love bite above the dimple in her ass. It's red but will probably be purple in a few hours. I make a mental note to myself that she bruises easily and I will need to be a little more careful next time.

Next time.

This is clearly not a one and done situation for me, nor can it be randomly casual. That's not who Adrienne is, and I don't think that's what I want from her. I think I want more.

I gently rise from the bed so I don't wake her to use the bathroom. I'm greeted at the doorway by her cat, Mittens, who rubs against my leg and purrs loudly. I bend down to scratch the top of her head. She's a beauty.

"My name's Jason," I tell her plainly because that's the way I talk to all animals. "It's nice to meet you. Can you show me around?"

The two of us walk around the living room and I take a careful look at everything hanging on Adrienne's walls. I'm in full belief that if you want to get to know someone, just take a look at the pictures, photographs and trinkets they used to decorate their home.

On one wall are photographs in assorted wooden frames of Adrienne and what looks like her mother, her father, and maybe friends from high school. I'm not sure she looks younger than how she appears today. In each photo she strikes a similar pose: smiling with her head slighted tilted to the side, always the left profile, always the light hitting her right above the cheekbone. There are quite a few pictures hung along the hallway, which lets me know she values family and her friendships. There's a genuine feeling of warmth you can see through her eyes in each photograph. If I had actually chosen Adrienne through a dating agency or app and had only these photos to go by, I know I would have picked her.

There's just something about her.

In the kitchen there are the typical small appliances you'd find such as a double slot toaster, blender, an air fryer and a wooden block of kitchen knives. There's a small shelf on the wall which holds a variety of cookbooks. One seems to be old and falling apart, perhaps a family heirloom. Some pages are tattered and some are clearly marked for further reference, like the page for smothered chicken. The others are all vegetarian cookbooks and look relatively new.

I want to toss them in the recycling bin.

I know they're there because of him.

There's a second smaller bedroom that Adrienne uses as her office. Inside there's a basic wooden desk with a vintage lamp and two tall bookshelves full of medical books. There's one sparse floor plant and a small eggplant-colored love seat. The decor is simple but functional and tells me a lot about who she is and what she treasures: comfort, practicality, simplicity.

I follow Mittens back into the bedroom where I look around to figure out where I will install her television. It can only go one place. Above a chest of drawers on the East wall. Luckily, there's a bracket that they sell at most large box stores I can use to install her television into the wall with only one hand and a power drill.

There are no pictures on the walls in here which tells

me that there were probably pictures of her and the ex somewhere and she's taken them down. Good. The last thing I need to see is a picture of his ugly mug when I'm making her come because I'm going to make her come again, and again, and again. I have so many more plans for Adrienne's body that I feel like a kid unwrapping a new toy on Christmas.

I sit on the edge of the bed beside her and stare at her like a lovesick teenager. Her eyelids periodically flutter like the wings of a dragonfly as she continues to peacefully rest.

In this state she looks very innocent, beautifully innocent, and I start to feel a twinge of guilt that I'm keeping who I really am from her. In fact, I don't know how long I'm going to be to keep this up. Already I want to spoil her with a gift or a weekend trip somewhere warm, but how would I explain that? With more lies? Like that I'm independently wealthy? Even if I did, someone would eventually recognize me. Hell, if we went to Times Square right now, she'd see for herself. There's an enormous billboard of me is up in lights advertising a sportswear brand I endorse.

It's settled. Now that our friendship has turned a corner, I'm going to have to tell her something, or tell her everything, and it needs to be today.

But first... breakfast.

TWENTY-SEVEN

ADRIENNE

SUNLIGHT WARMS my bare breasts as I yawn in complete and utter exhaustion and satisfaction. I had some of the best sex of my life last night. The kind that raunchy R&B groups sing about. The kind that *almost* makes me want to rent Jason out and show all of my friends what they're missing. The kind that makes me think about crazy stuff, like how much it would cost to throw a wedding in Bali. The kind that makes me want to go at it again, right this very minute.

I feel the other side of the bed with my palm and it's cold. Jason isn't here and evidently hasn't been in bed for a while. For just a moment, I panic. I wonder if perhaps he got what he wanted from me and left, or if the intensity of our lovemaking frightened him away because if I'm going to be honest, that shit was scary. Scary good. He chased away any bad juju I thought this bed or bedroom would have forever.

I've spent most of my adult life believing that either something was wrong with me or that people were lying. Sex has never been fantastic or life changing for me. It's just been something I did when I was in a serious relationship with a man because that's what you do, right? Sure, the foreplay was nice and being held afterwards was always lovely, but the actual act was anticlimactic.

Last night was different.

Last night was a freakin' erogenous zone masterclass. Jason taught me things about my body that I didn't know, and I'm a damn doctor. And the awesome thing about it was that he never made me feel silly or uncomfortable or inept. In fact, all that I felt last night was adored and orgasmic and powerful.

I grab my cell to see if maybe my new sex sensei left me a text explaining his sudden disappearance and audibly gasp at how many missed calls I have.

Twenty-four missed calls over the last hour and none of them are from work? Most of the calls are from numbers I don't recognize, but the last caller I do and he had the nerve to leave a message.

"Why aren't you picking up the phone, Adrienne? Are you with him right now? Are you fucking him right now? Is this your revenge? He's using you. Call me back right fucking now!"

It's Troy, and he sounds like a complete lunatic. I definitely dodged a bullet when he decided to blow up our relationship into tiny little bits. I'm not even going to dignify his irate voice message with a response. He's just trying to get a reaction from me because Jason tossed him out on his ass last night, but I will not give him one.

My phone rings again, but this time it's Dena. I'm sure she's calling to ask me how the second date went so she can check in with Caroline.

"Hey, I–"

"Adrienne!"

"What?"

"Oh my bejeezus, Adrienne!"

"What?!"

"Don't play stupid with me."

"I'm not playing dumb. What's wrong with you, nutball?"

"What's wrong is that my best friend is on every gossip blog on the planet and I'm the last to know. Seriously, A, it's embarrassing. Everyone's asking me for details and I don't even have a clue what they're talking about."

"Dena, I need you to take a breath and explain yourself."

"Oh ok, so this is how you're going to play it? All cool and shit."

"You've known me long enough to know that I don't play games. Hell, I don't even know how to play games. So cut the crap and just tell me what you're accusing me of?"

"I'm accusing you of being a really rotten friend and not giving me all the tea about your dates. I'm the one that hooked it up! How dare you not tell me that Caroline arranged for you to date the quarterback of The

New York Nighthawks! You and Jett freaking Caraway are all over social media. ”

"You're mistaken, best friend." Her accusation is hilarious. "I'm dating a starving artist named Jason."

"No, Boo, you're dating a millionaire named Jason *Jett* Caraway. Woo-hoo!" She exclaims. "You really hit the jackpot with that one, A. Talk about leveling up."

My stomach churns with disappointment.

What Dena's saying sounds so ridiculous yet makes complete sense. The constant stares. Jason's major injury. The out-of-the-way restaurants that gave us the best service I've ever seen. The flower bouquets that even I couldn't afford. The intricate tattoo of a jet plane in flight on his back.

Jett.

He lied to me.

That mother humper lied to me.

"I'll call you back."

I hang up on Dena and open all of my social media Apps. I'm not even sure what I'm looking for, but I remember what Dena said and type the search term, New York Nighthawks.

And that's when I see it.

The first thing that comes up on my feed is a picture of Jason and me from last night in front of my apartment building hauling the television set inside. They conveniently cropped the Uber driver, who helped us out of the picture. Under the photograph is a caption that reads:

Jason Jett Caraway and Mystery Woman Moving In Together?

It's a simple enough click-bait headline, but the story which follows is another matter. It basically suggests that his "affair" with me may be the reason why an entire football team is not winning this season.

Holy crap.

I'm startled out of my daze when the phone rings again and it's my cousin Carline. She's a cousin on my father's side of the family, and the two of us don't normally chat. In fact, I haven't seen her since the last Hodges family wedding. The only reason she would be calling me is because she knows something about this and wants to confirm that this picture is the real deal. I ignore the call but notice a new text from her.

Carline: Is that my little cousin making out with a baller from the Nighthawks? WOW! Can you get me tickets to a game and does he have a friend?

If she knows about this headline, my entire family knows, which means that it won't be long before my mother decides to call and that's not a conversation I'm looking forward to having. Can you imagine?

Are you dating a football player now, hun?

Oh no, Mom, I just fucked him all night to help eradicate the memories of Troy fucking another woman in my house.

Yeah, this is a certifiable nightmare.

I just spread my legs for another liar, and now the entire world knows. I'm a total book smart but not street smart cliche. I look like a complete idiot.

I guess I have my answer on where he's disappeared

to. He probably saw my phone blowing up and got out of dodge fast. The jerk didn't even have the decency to stay and man up to his deception.

I can't believe I thought he was destitute.

I was going to help him apply for a series of grants the hospital gives to surgical candidates who need financial help.

Am I the most naïve woman who walked the earth?

I click on a hyperlink of Jason's name and am redirected to another article. This one is more thorough and less gossipy. It gives details about his career, including his illustrious time playing in college and his accomplishments and troubles in the NFL. It also lists some celebrities he's dated (including one of the Kardashians) and his net worth, which is a little over... sixty-two million dollars?!

My phone slips from my hand and drops to the floor. I'm in shock.

What was a millionaire ball player doing in my bed last night? What probable motive could he have for sleeping with me when he can have any woman he wants? The answer is simple. There is no complicated motive or goal. I was a warm body, for one night, for one cold-blooded asshole.

That's it, and that's all.

My nude body shivers, but not from the temperature of the room, but because I'm incensed. I'm almost hyperventilating under the weight of my covers when I hear the lock on the front door click open.

It can't be him.

It better not be him.
Where the hell is my baseball bat?

TWENTY-EIGHT

JETT

IT'S ALMOST as if there's a stranger inside of my body. Like one of those lame fictional characters in a rom-com movie who aimlessly skips around bumbling through the day because he just found the right one but doesn't know it quite yet.

I've always believed that my father cheated on my mom because he made a promise to her he was incapable of keeping. Why else would he and half the rest of the world commit adultery, hurting people they care about? If human beings had a better understanding of what they can and cannot do and be honest about it, I swear the world would be a better place.

I have always prided myself on knowing myself well. My strengths. My limitations. I know that I am in a position to really hurt someone if I'm not careful, which is why I pick a certain type of woman to get involved with and am always honest about what we're doing. It protects us both.

But now I'm doubting everything I've ever believed. Is it possible that Adrienne is my rom-com girl? The one woman to make me change my entire belief system about relationships. It's the only thing that would explain how I'm feeling about her.

My wish to protect her.

My need to make her laugh.

The gratification I feel when I feed her.

My desire to be inside of her.

The craving to own every part of her.

She differs completely from any other woman I have known. Some men in the league only want a woman who other men will envy because of her looks, and I used to be no different, but I feel like I hit the jackpot with Adrienne. Not only is she any man's wet dream, but she's also smart as fuck and her career gives her an immense sense of purpose. Not a lot of players can say that about their women. Not a lot of them even care about that. But I obviously do, because I find both her brains and her butt a turn on in a way that I've never been before.

Then there are the innocent parts of Adrienne. I didn't let her know because there was no need to tell her, but it was obvious she had little to no experience riding a man. But that shit turned me on even more. I may or may not have been her first ride, but I damn sure was her best and she was mine.

Hell, that pussy has magical healing powers because by the time we were finished last night, I was completely wiped and fell asleep before midnight for the first time since I broke my collarbone. For me, that is pretty close to a Christmas miracle.

Of course, if I had known she fibbed about being on top as her favorite position, I would have planned the evening a little differently. I was pulling out all my tricks from the start so she would quickly forget how she was humiliated inside of that room by her ex. In hindsight, I made some assumptions that I shouldn't have and we could have taken things slower. Fortunately, I can make up for that blunder when I get back.

When I woke up this morning, Adrienne was sleeping peacefully buck naked and beautiful under the covers. I've been fantasizing the last thirty minutes about how many more things I can teach her and how many more ways I will pleasure her.

Hell, I don't care what we do as long as the day ends with her wrapped around me like a hot blanket, squeezing me dry and begging for mercy.

I saw little in Adrienne's fridge this morning, so I wanted to grab the essentials. Even with one hand I can still make her a veggie scramble, some sausage and maybe a bagel on the side.

The plan is to feed her, fuck her, and then spend the rest of the day figuring out how to get that damn TV screen on the wall with one hand and without calling Bryan to help me. He'd give my ass away for sure.

I use the spare key I made Troy leave behind to let myself back in the apartment. I'm not sure that I trust that these are his only copies, so I have plans to get Adrienne's locks changed too.

I chuckle inside.

I guess I've got a lot of plans for her.

Once I let myself in the apartment, I'm faced by a very anguished Adrienne standing under the doorway of her bedroom.

Phone in her hand.

Tears streaming down her face.

Seeing her upset like this makes me feel like I've been shanked in my side. The pain is sharp and harsh.

She knows.

"Evidently you are quite the famous quarterback."

"Let me explain."

"I thought you were a starving artist?"

"I never said that."

"You said you were a painter," she scoffs.

"I said that while I had time off, I was painting, which is true."

"Where do you paint?"

"In my house?"

"Which is where?"

I hesitate because I don't want to tell her about my mom, but I've got a feeling that she's been looking me up in her phone for the last twenty minutes. She probably knows everything, and now I'm being tested.

"The East Side on 66th."

"Square footage?"

"4200 square feet."

"Articles are pretty accurate then." She exaggerates her point by scrolling through the many pages of my life in print on her phone. "That must have cost you a pretty penny."

Fuck, she's livid.

"I need to explain, Adrienne."

"You realize that you're just as bad as he is, right?"

"Are we *still* talking about that piece of shit?" I instinctually move closer to her. "I would never disrespect you like he did. Ever."

"You just did."

"There were reasons for keeping my identity quiet."

"It doesn't matter what they are."

My stomach churns again. She's not budging.

"Adrienne–"

"When were you going to tell me?"

I get even closer to her so that she can feel the regret pouring off of me.

"Last night was so perfect that I didn't want to ruin it."

"It's not only ruined, but it's already forgotten."

Ouch, that hurt, but I realize that was the intention. I'm not giving up on her or on us, not when I've just found her.

I slide my hand along the side of her face into her hair.

Her eyes close for just a moment.

I take a momentary small comfort in knowing that her body is in conflict with her brain. She wants to hear me out, but her pride won't let her. Then a trash that selfish thought and recognize the distress I am causing her. I've never regretted a poor decision as much as I do right now.

She takes what seems like a deep cleansing breath, opens her eyes, and stares me straight on.

"I never want to see you again, Jason."

There's a gut wrenching pain I suffer from her words because I know she means them, and it hurts worse than any damage a player could ever do to me on the football field. Lucky for me, I've been battled tested. I'm not giving up on her or on the possibility of us.

Not without a fight.

TWENTY-NINE

ADRIENNE

"DR. HODGES, there's a new patient here to see you without an appointment."

"Is it an emergency, Penny?"

"I don't think so."

"So can you just reschedule them please?"

"Um, I tried to, but the guardian won't take no for an answer."

"Seriously? I don't need any parent drama. I'm swamped today."

"He promises it will just take a second. I promised him you could take a look."

"Why did you promise that? Is he a friend of yours?"

"No, but–"

I practically slam down my paperwork on the desk and walk away from Penny with heavy steps into the waiting room.

"That's them," Penny points with a grin.

There's a little girl with two fuzzy pigtails and a runny nose playing with a doll, and her "guardian" greets me with hopeful silver eyes.

"Hi, beautiful."

"This is a low even for you."

He bows his head in what clearly must be shame. Where on earth did he get this little girl from?

I crouch down to face my new little patient.

"And who are you?"

"I'm Janet."

"Hi Janet, I'm doctor Hodges."

"It's a pleasure to make your acquaintance."

I raise my eyebrows and look at Jason for an explanation as to why this little girl sounds like she's straight out of a period drama.

"She watches a lot of public television."

I turn my lips up.

"Well, it's a pleasure to make your acquaintance as well. Are you feeling a little sick today?"

"Yes, Mommy says I have a bad cold."

Oh my God, it just hit me. Could this little girl be Jason's child?

I cut my eyes at him suspiciously as I continue talking to Janet.

"And so Daddy brought you to the doctor's office to get checked out?"

Janet giggles as she wraps one of the doll's curls around her finger.

"Daddy's at work. This is my big brother, Jett."

I'm both relieved and shocked, although I shouldn't be surprised that I didn't know that Jason had a sister. I pretty much just slept with a stranger, so of course I'm learning new things about him every single minute.

"Your brother?"

"My father remarried," he explains delicately. "This is his stepdaughter, Janet… my new sister."

I know how Jason feels about his father, so it's nice to see that he at least has a relationship with his stepsister, but bringing her here as an excuse to see me isn't cool. You don't use a child like that.

"Penny, can you put them in room seven and I'll see her as soon as I'm finished with the Dawson family?"

"Sure thing."

I almost choke on my saliva as Penny bats her eyes adoringly at Jason. I've never seen her act like that in the years that I've known her, and we've had some pretty hot dads come through these doors. I guess seeing a football superstar up close and personal like Jason is a little different from gawking at a halfway hot soccer dad. It's as if he's completely hypnotized our normally very grounded head of nursing. Actually, now that I look around, he's memorized the entire room. Moms are smoothing their hair back and texting on their phones, no doubt telling their friends who they've spotted in the waiting area.

I stop at my office for a moment to catch my breath. I wasn't expecting to see Jason at all again, much less here at work, and I will not lie he looks hella hot. He's wearing a pair of well-worn jeans, a cream Polo sweater, and dark brown boots.

Damn, he's playing dirty.

I knock three times before I enter the room. Janet is

sitting on the examining table swinging her little legs back and forth and Jason's massive physique is awkwardly trying to get comfortable in a plastic chair that's two sizes too small for him. His face beams when I enter the room, and it takes everything in me not to smile in return. I've missed him, I'm very much attracted to him, but I can't ever trust him. I just can't do it.

I roll my eyes for dramatic effect and shove a clipboard into his chest with some intake paperwork. "Fill these out," I tell him sternly.

"Yes, Ma'm." He smirks.

I squirt some sanitizer on my hands and turn my attention to my new little patient and smile.

"How long have you had this cold, Janet?"

"About three days," he answers for her.

I pause and exhale dramatically, then I address Janet again.

"Lets check your temperature, ok?"

She nods excitedly

I proceed with the typical examination I'd give a sick patient and verify that Janet has a simple cold with no fever and will get better with frequent liquids and a few days in bed. I wonder if her mother even knows that he brought her here. She's fine.

"Is there a nice doctor who mommy or daddy takes you to, Janet? I'm asking because I want to be sure to let him know that I've seen you today and what your symptoms were."

"Well, she-" he attempts to answer for her again.

"I'd like Janet to answer, please."

"She's only six."

"And probably has been talking since she was two. Go ahead, Janet."

"Mommy takes me to see Doctor Kinney sometimes. She gives me shots though."

I cock my head to the side at Jason.

"Is that so?"

"I realize she has a regular pediatrician, but you were close by," he uses as a lame excuse. "We were at the zoo."

"You took her to the zoo, and she's had a cold for three days?"

He shrugs his shoulders. "I thought she was over it."

"You finished with those forms?" I ask icily.

"Um, no."

"Well, you and Janet are finished here and we need the room, so take them back out to the front and finish them there. I have another patient waiting for me."

I reach out to shake Janet's hand.

"It was lovely to meet you, Janet."

"The pleasure was all mine."

I giggle to myself. She's more polite than my Grandma Jane."

"Wait, is that it?" Jason asks with fear in his voice.

"Yes, that's it. I gave her a complete examination, and she's fine. Nothing's wrong that a little rest and chicken soup won't cure."

"But Jet promised me McDonalds if we went to the doctor's not soup." Janet pouts.

My eyes cut over to him again.

"You were promised fries, huh, Janet?"

"With chicken nuggets too!"

I shake my head in obvious disapproval, although secretly I'm giving him points for effort.

"Unbelievable."

He shrugs his shoulders and flashes me that signature Jason smile.

"This is what groveling is supposed to look like, baby."

He's seriously testing my resolve.

"Bye."

When I return home that evening, my plan is to jump in the tub and read one of my historical novels to give my brain a break from the medical books until I hear a knock at the door.

I look through the peephole and there's a man with a slight build and red hair patiently waiting with some sort of bag in his hand.

"Who is it?"

"Hi, I'm Bryan. I'm here to install your television."

"I don't have a tv."

"I'm not trying to freak you out, Miss Hodges, but I work for Mr. Caraway. He sent me over to install the television."

Of course.

"You work for him?"

"I'm his personal assistant."

Wow.

"And he sent you here to hang my television on the wall?"

"Yes, he did."

"You can tell him I don't need his help. I've got the situation taken care of."

"He told me you'd say that and he told me if you did I should text him, which I did, and now he wants you to check your cell phone."

My phone vibrates against the granite countertop of my kitchen.

Gah! This man.

Jason: I have instructed Bryan to wait in front of your door until you let him in to do what I have paid him to do. He will wait there all night if he has to.

Me: You think this impressive? Putting your employees to work like this?

Jason: I'd do it myself, but you know how that will turn out. Someone will post a picture of me in front of your house online in an hour. Just trying to respect your privacy AND stick to my word.

Me: This changes nothing. I just don't want this poor guy to sit out here all night.

Jason: Great! I'll let him know you'll be letting him in. It will only take him about thirty minutes, tops.

Me: Goodbye, Jason.

Jason: Dream of me tonight, beautiful.

I open my door to let the assistant in.

"Hi, I'm Adrienne."

"And I'm sorry."

I giggle.

"Can I get you something to drink or a snack before you get started? I'm not sure it's fair that you have to do this. I would've said no if I didn't actually believe he'd leave you outside my door all night."

"Oh, he definitely would, so I thank you for kindly **acquiescing**."

"What's it like working for a man like Jason?"

"An adventure every day."

"Have you had to do things like this before?"

"Not for a woman."

"Did he tell you to say that?" I ask, unconvinced.

"He pays me to work, but I do all of my own thinking for free."

I giggle again.

"You're funny, Bryan."

"And you're very much as he described."

"What's that?"

"Beautiful on the inside and out."

ADRIENNE

WHEN MY MOTHER and I plan a mother and daughter shopping excursion, we always make a day out of it. It always begins with breakfast at our favorite pancake house, then we shop for what could very well be hours and finally we end the afternoon with a musical (or some sort of other old movie) at home on the couch or we pull out the photo albums and look at old pictures of dad. It really depends upon her mood and how much time I have.

Today we're shopping for Cecily's wedding and we have several things on the list to purchase. The first thing I need is a pair of shoes to go with my bridesmaid's dress and you guessed it, the dress is the color blush pink. I also need a flesh-colored pair of Spanx to hold in all of my jiggly parts, and finally I need to purchase a gift for the happy couple. I do not know what I'm going to get them, but mom assures me that there's plenty to choose from her five wedding registries.

Talk about overkill.

"Right this way, ladies."

After the hostess seats us, my mom pulls out a travel pack of wipes and wipes down the table.

"They've got people who do that you know?"

"Wipe our table with that dirty dish water they use? No, thank you."

"Do you want to stop coming here if you're concerned about the cleanliness of the place? Maybe find another breakfast spot? There are plenty in this city."

"It's the same no matter where we go, sweetie, so we might as well stay here where we can at least be guaranteed that the food is good."

My mother is one of a kind. Some things that she rationalizes make little sense, but that's one thing that makes her different from her twin, Aunt Lorraine. They may look identical and finish each other's sentences, but in many ways they are very different.

After we put in our orders with the server—who gives us the side eye for wiping down a table she's already cleaned—the inquisition begins. I haven't had a chance to talk to my mom in person since the news bite broke about me and Jason, and naturally she has questions.

"I've been waiting to see you in person to talk about what's going on in your personal life. Both sides of the family are talking about it and have called me for information. They wanted to know what it's like to meet a superstar such as this Jett person, and of course I had to tell them I knew nothing about him. It was embarrassing to say the least, sweetie."

"Imagine my embarrassment," I mutter under my breath.

"I suppose I shouldn't be too shocked that I haven't met him yet. My daughter likes to keep her men far away from her family."

"That's not true," I protest.

"It took you three months to introduce me to Troy."

"It took me three months to introduce you two because it was like pulling teeth to get him to agree to it. He was supposedly so busy with this or that, but the truth is he never felt that meeting my family was a priority. He just didn't care."

"But we met him several times. He was so nice."

"Yes, but it took a lot of strong arming for us to get to that point. He was polite because he knows how to work a room, not necessarily because he genuinely liked you all."

"Oh." My mother looks visibly disappointed.

"I'm sorry, Mom, but Troy deceived me in the worst way. He was not who he claimed to be. Without getting into the gory details, he cheated and lied and I would never want to resume a relationship with him in this life or the next."

"Well agreed. It's over. I didn't realize how strongly you felt about the breakup. I thought it was just a lover's spat."

"I realize that and I should have explained earlier, but it was just still so raw."

The server brings our food in record time. Mom

ordered her usual western omelet and coffee, and I ordered a short stack with sausage links.

"You ordered sausage?"

"I missed the little stinkers," I say comically.

"I see," she responds as she watches me take a bite with great enthusiasm. "Welcome back to the dark side."

We both chuckle out loud and it feels good to laugh again.

"So when am I going to meet this hot shot quarterback you're dating now?"

The laughs abruptly end.

"You're not."

"And why not?"

"He came in my life unexpectedly. In fact, I met him the night I broke up with Troy. It probably wasn't the greatest time to meet someone, and my guard was down. I didn't know who he was when we met, and he conveniently decided not to tell me."

My mother pensively chews a bite of her eggs and then speaks again.

"I imagine that his life is quite difficult."

"Really, Mom? He's rich, he's famous, and he's good looking. I think his life is a cakewalk."

"Many people think your life has been easy too, but no one really understands the hours of hard work you have put into graduating high school early, finishing college in four years with all those hard science classes you had, and don't even get me started on medical school. People do not know the sacrifice it takes to achieve a goal like that. They think, oh that Adrienne girl is super smart. Things are easy for her."

She may have a point, but so what.

"And before you go judging him harshly, your aunt told me he hasn't been having an easy time of it here in New York."

"Which is ridiculous. How could that article say I'm the reason why he got hurt? We didn't even know each other then."

"Exactly, which proves my point. They've been gunning for him long before he ever met you. Your aunt said that the entire city wants someone named Rivera to play and never wanted him here. That must have been really hard, to move to a place where nobody wants you."

Now she's making my pancakes taste funny. They feel like little boulders sliding down my throat and settling hard into my stomach.

"Do you and Aunt Lorraine talk about everything?" I whine.

"Not everything."

"Mom, the bottom line is he lied to me and I just can't do it all over again. I just got out of a relationship with a liar. I'd be stupid to start anything with him."

"Sounds like it's already started."

"Nothing real has started. I was basically getting to know a complete stranger."

"Or maybe you were getting to know the actual person. The person he is without football. Maybe that's who he wanted you to meet."

"But being a football player is a huge part of who he is, so in my opinion, I don't know him at all."

I lay down my fork.

"This conversation is ruining my pancake breakfast."

"The trouble with him seems to bother you way more than the end of your engagement did."

"Why would you think that?" I respond incredulously.

"Because if my engagement to your father ended, I would have been under the bed for a month. You seemed to have shaken yours off and moved on pretty quickly."

I take another struggle bite of my pancakes and shrug my shoulders.

"I can't grieve for something that didn't exist."

"And what about your quarterback, are you grieving over him?"

I feel a squeeze in my chest.

"No."

"Mmm, ok.

I know what that means. My mother is not buying what I'm saying for one second, but I'm a firm believer that you can speak whatever you want into existence if you say it enough.

I do not miss Jason Jett Caraway.

I do not miss Jason.

I do not miss him.

Fuck.

THIRTY-ONE

ADRIENNE

WHEN DENA WALKS into my house, she immediately scrunches up her nose.

"Your house smells like the floral palace on Elm Street."

There are bouquets of freesias, orchids, roses, lilies, hydrangeas and peonies all over my living room. They keep coming. Day after day, Jason sends me a floral arrangement. He won't stop. I would give some to the neighbors, but I barely know them. It got so annoying I texted him, but soon realized that's exactly what he wanted.

Me: Stop sending me all these dead plants.
Jason: You don't like them?
Me: NO!
Jason: I thought you said you liked flowers.
Me: You never asked me that.

Jason: Flowers or Candy, then?
Me: Neither
Jason: More flowers or a third date?
Me: I'm not playing this game with you.
Jason: Then go drink because you probably need a cocktail right about now, don't you? I bet it's hard recollecting all day, every day, about how good it felt when I was so deep inside your pussy that you couldn't think straight.

Me: You are a nut job.

Jason: I've never heard a woman come so loudly in my life. Admit you love this Texas dick. Riding me reverse cowboy like a fucking champion. I'm hard just thinking about it.

I went radio silent after that because I spent the next fifteen minutes in bed with my vibrator, reliving exactly every dirty word he sent in his text message. And almost like he knew, he sent me one more message later that night.

Me: Good night, beautiful. I hope you came hard. I know I did.

"Be quiet and come in," I tell Dena.

"Caroline wants to meet you."

I look at Dena like she just bumped her head.

"And why would either of us want to do that?"

"Because her unsatisfied client demands it."

This man.

"What did he say to her? He didn't even pay for the

match. This was a favor on both of our parts. What demands could he possibly be making?"

"He wrote her a check to pay for the match like any other client."

"When?"

"Yesterday."

"How much was it?"

"One-hundred and fifty thousand dollars."

"What?! You have got to be kidding me, Dena."

"I swear that's the going rate for a high-end match. Women pay less, of course. There's a method to their madness, I suppose."

"I can't even believe I let you talk me into participating in such an archaic system to begin with. Men and women should just meet the old-fashioned way."

"Oh, like at a bar? Lets not get into that debate again. What's done is done. You've already agreed to the terms, went on two dates, and owe Jett and the agency another one."

"I sure hope that Caroline's donation is worth it to you because you are about to lose one best friend over it."

"Settle down, A. So what, you didn't know that he was a franchise quarterback for the Nighthawks. This is some Cinderella shit you're living right now. Your brainy ass got the prince. You should be ecstatic that you hit it off with someone like Jett Caraway. I mean damn."

"You mean I should be grateful."

"There you go, twisting my words again. I didn't say that."

"Are you on my side or not, Dena?"

"Of course I'm always on your side. That should go without saying. But I don't really understand why there are sides. I really don't."

"Jason had plenty of opportunities to tell me who he was and chose not to. I can't trust someone who's just going to pick and choose what basic things they decide to share with me about their lives."

"What did you want him to do? Was he just supposed to blurt out who he was in the middle of the Wild Boar?! Trust me when I say there would have been pandemonium."

"Or how about he could have mentioned it when he was in between my legs!"

"Aaah!" Dena snaps her fingers in front of my face. Something she does when she's excited or has an aha moment. "You conveniently left out all the juicy parts. You slept with him?!"

"Unfortunately."

"Was it good?"

It was fantastic.

"Perhaps."

She smiles broader.

"Was he humongous? I mean, he has to be one of the biggest quarterbacks in the league."

I roll my eyes at her crassness.

"What do you think?"

"I think he definitely was. I think he was so good that you're thinking about it right now."

"Get out of my house," I (sort of) jest.

"This explains so much. That's why you're so angry."

"I admit that the fact we were intimate plays a bit of

role in why I feel so betrayed. I really revealed and shared a part of myself with him that night. I can't say that he did the same. I feel stupid."

"But did he make you come though?"

I throw one of my couch pillows at her head.

"I'm proud of you best friend because you must have put it on him. He's coming at you from all angles. I take it the flowers are from him?"

"Yes, and the other day he showed up at my job unannounced."

"He just popped by?"

"With a child."

She snaps her fingers again.

"Ooh, that's gangster! Did he hire a child actor or something? I bet he did."

"No, Dena, of course not. She's his sister."

"Oh, I didn't know he had a sister. His Wikipedia says he's an only child."

"She's his stepsister from his dad's relatively new marriage."

"Ahh, so you do know insider stuff."

"So what does Caroline want to say to me?"

"She wants to beg for you to reconsider. Jett is willing to be a part of a whole promotion for her company if she can get you to agree to the third date."

"That's unfortunate for her then because there's not a chance in hell I'm going out with him again."

"Is that your final answer?"

"What is this, Jeopardy? Yes."

"Then you won't be angry if she matches him with someone else?"

"Someone else?"

"Well, yeah, the money he paid is for an annual membership. If one match doesn't work out, then he can meet another woman."

That asshole!

"Hell yeah," I tell Dena. "In fact, I recommend that Caroline find him another match. We're just not compatible. It's not happening."

"Fine, I'll let her know."

"Why do you sound so disappointed?"

"I think you are making a major mistake."

"I make 'em all the time. I'll live with it."

I try studying for an hour, but it's a waste of time. I keep being drawn to my laptop and the search engine bar. I look up Jason and try to create a timeline of his alleged relationships and celebrity dalliances over the years. I actually write them down on a piece of paper and study the dates. It looks like he spent the most time with an actress I've seen in all of maybe three movies.

I click on her name, which is linked to a Wikipedia page as well. Under her personal section, it says that she was in a relationship with Jason Jett Caraway on and off for a year. There's even a picture of them walking hand in hand on a beach.

That leads me down another rabbit hole for an hour or so because now I want to know more. I find little, which in some ways disappoints me. There isn't much to find online because his association with this woman was obviously very casual. And this was his longest documented relationship?

What a joke.

THIRTY-TWO

ADRIENNE

I HAVE a study group tonight at Owen's place and I'm looking forward to it. Nothing can get my mind off of things I'm stressed about better than working towards a goal. Getting my board certification in pediatrics will be just one more solid step towards meeting my career goals, which include securing a permanent position in Mercy West's pediatric clinic and one day teaching.

When the four of us meet at Owen's apartment to study, it's always my responsibility to bring the coffee, so I stop at the local coffee shop to grab a to-go carton of dark roast and some assorted pasties. I'm pleased to see one of the regular baristas there who I'm friendly with, but our jovial chit-chat quickly turns when he tells me that his cancer has returned.

The barista is only twenty-three years old, and this will be his second battle with bone cancer. It's so unfair. He's a nice guy who just wants to live the rest of his life like everybody else. I try giving him one of my mini motivational speeches about how I'm so sure that he'll beat his cancer again because of the kind he has and his age, but I'm not as confident about things as I hopefully appeared. After I leave, his news darkens my mood so much that I hardly notice when a shiny black SUV abruptly stops next to me as I walk toward Owen's.

It's him.

"Where are you going this time of night?"

His unexpected appearance and the tone of his voice throws me off and only sours my mood.

"None of your business."

"We have one more date."

"Go away." I continue to walk.

"You signed a contract."

He snatches the carton of coffee out of my hand, and we keep walking. The SUV trails slowly behind us and I realize it must not be a regular Uber car but one of Jason's. God knows he's rich enough to own a fleet of cars.

"Is that your car?" I ask.

"Yes."

"Do you have a driver too?"

"Sometimes."

"Caroline can tear up the contract and give you your money back. Oh wait, that's right, she can find you another match."

"I don't want another match. I want my third date with you, Adrienne."

"Well, I want world peace and healthcare for all, but that ain't happening no time soon."

"What's wrong with you today? Did something happen at work?"

"You're what's wrong."

"So let me understand something. You were actually considering getting back with that asshole after he fucked someone in your bed and you won't give me a pass because I didn't tell you what I do for a living?"

The way he brought up Troy and what he did is painful. His choice of words and the tone in which he delivered them are caustic, and they hurt me almost as much as if he physically slapped me.

"You're a liar just like him."

"I am *nothing* like him."

At this point we are in front of Owen's place. Owen lives on the first floor of a brownstone and can hear everything that happens outside in the front half of his apartment where we usually study. He opens the heavy wood door to his place in his shirt and basketball shorts, looking meaner than he really is.

"Everything okay out here?" he asks sternly.

I think everyone who matters in my life (and thousands who don't) now know that I have some sort of association with Jett Caraway, but they don't know the details because no one dares to ask me (except for my family). I don't bring it up and they don't ask. Even if they did, I would refuse to talk about it, but that doesn't mean that they can't read. Owen knows exactly who Jason is and from what I know is a big sports fan, but that doesn't matter right now. He's got my back as a friend and I appreciate that more than he knows right now.

"Everything's fine, Owen. Are Paige and Keisha here yet?"

"No, they're running a little late."

Jason extends his hand.

"Hi, I'm Jett."

It's so weird to hear him introduce himself as Jett, but that's his name. I'm the only dummy who it sounds odd to.

"I know who you are," Owen says, and neither Jason nor I miss the edge to his tone. He's being an ass for my sake, but he may overdo it a bit.

"It's nice to meet you." Jason continues with the pleasantries, not taking the bait.

"Uh huh," Owen says dismissively. "We should probably get going, A. We've got a lot of work to do tonight."

This is getting uncomfortable. I know that Owen probably senses the tension between Jason and me and is only trying to help, but I can feel Jason's blood boiling. He doesn't like Owen already, and this can only go in one direction at this point... south.

"She's not going anywhere until we're finished talking," Jason says.

"Wait-" I try putting an end to this but Owen over talks me.

"What you and Adrienne are going through is none of my business, but she's my friend and I know she isn't comfortable right now, which means that I'm uncomfortable."

"Is that fucking right? Damn, Adrienne, you have a

lot of men in your life that are always trying to talk to you when I'm around."

"Listen man, maybe you call the shots in the locker room and on the field, but right now you're in front of my house. This is my ball game. And you're harassing one of my friends. So you need to go before I call the police."

The police?

Okay, wait, this is getting out of hand. I've never seen this side of Owen. I've only ever thought of him as a reliable study buddy, but now I see his value as a genuine friend. Someone willing to stick up for me just in case I need a little backup, albeit a little too zealously.

"Thanks, Owen, but Jett (I can't believe I just called him that) and I were just finishing up a little conversation that was long overdue. I'll be up in three minutes."

"You sure?"

He touches my shoulder.

"Yes, thanks."

Jason laughs cynically as Owen returns inside the house. Then he paces back and forth in front of me like a maniac who gulped down too many energy drinks.

"What?!"

"You're giving me three goddamn minutes?"

"Watch your mouth and I'm here to study, not chop it up with you."

"Are you fucking him?"

"What did you just ask me?"

"Are you sleeping with that prick?"

"I'm not going to even dignify that with an answer. Go home."

His eyes look panicked.

"I'm sorry. I didn't mean that. I don't know what I'm saying."

"You're right, you don't. I'm going in the house, Jason. You need to leave."

"I just miss you so damn much."

Why can't I just confess? I miss him too.

"We haven't even known each other that long. Just go back to doing whatever you were doing before you met me."

"That's the thing, beautiful, I wasn't doing a fucking thing, and I didn't even realize it. I was just passing time before I met you."

My head drops.

"You made me cry."

"What?" He lifts my head to meet his gaze.

"I said that I would never cry over a man and you made me cry."

"I promise that I'll never make you cry again."

"You can't promise that."

"I swear it, Adrienne."

Of course he can't promise me that. That's why I shouldn't stand out here any longer listening to him. The problem is that I want him to say something... anything that will make the last few weeks ago away. I wish more than anything that we could start all over that day in the Wild Boar, but we can't, and I'm not even sure if we did that anything would have happened differently.

I'm torturing myself for even daring to dream that something could happen between me and Jason. He hid himself from me for a reason. His life differs completely from mine and certainly bigger than mine. I don't want to date a celebrity; I don't want to be photographed; I don't want my entire life documented, and I definitely don't want to watch him get his brains bashed out every Sunday.

No, I made the right decision.

The two of us just can't work.

"I've got to go, Jason. It's getting cold out here."

"We can sit in the car and talk for a little while longer."

I look up at Owen's living room window and look over at Jason's car. Something is pulling me toward the car, toward Jason, toward hearing him out for a little longer — but I know I'd just be setting myself up. Once I got in that car, I'd never leave. If I'm ever going to stop repeating the mistakes of my past, then it starts here.

The relationship I thought I was starting was all in my head with a fictitious starving artist, not the man standing before me right now.

He pulls my icy hand into his large, warm one.

"Just five minutes."

He pulls me closer, and I let him. I haven't been this close to him in what feels like forever, but has only been a few weeks.

He leans his forehead into mine and closes his eyes. There's a quiet between us that's filled with beeping horns, voices of passerby's, and other noises of the city.

"Five minutes," he says again, and the warmth of his breath warms my skin.

Suddenly my lips part as if they have a mind and need of their own, but just before he seals my mouth with his own, Paige and Keisha approach us. They've arrived from the subway exit at Owen's corner.

"Adrienne?"

When they see who I'm standing with, they both suddenly make gobsmacked apologies.

"Oh, we're so sorry."

"Damn, it's Jett Caraway."

"We shouldn't have interrupted."

"Go back to what you were doing. So sorry."

Once they scamper away and enter Owen's vestibule, I start to slowly back away from Jason.

"Baby-" he pleads.

"I gotta go."

I run away from Jason and up Owen's steps at breakneck speed.

This has been the hardest goodbye to date.

I hope it's the last.

I might not survive another one.

ADRIENNE

"WHO GETS MARRIED ON THANKSGIVING DAY?" Dena fusses as she helps me blow out my hair. "We should all be sitting around the table eating turkey, macaroni and cheese and watching–"

She stops herself.

"You can say it," I tell her.

"Watching football," she hesitantly finishes her sentence. "Sorry, A."

It's been several weeks since I've seen or heard from Jason. He's been in and out-of-town traveling with the Nighthawks as they continue playing their season. Even though he's on injured reserved, as quarterback of the team it's still his job to be at all games, helping the backup quarterback with plays and whatever else Dena tried to explain to me he does.

Today they are away in Texas playing Dallas, and I imagine while he's there he'll visit his family because of the holiday. I don't expect to hear from him, and I'd feel a little silly at this point reaching out to him. I was the one so adamant about him leaving me alone, only to regret that he's finally listening to what I asked for.

"Dena, stop pulling so hard, you're going to make me bald."

"I mean, is Cecily going to have little paper turkeys as centerpieces? What the hell? This was not her smartest idea."

"I'm pretty sure there aren't any paper turkeys. Her color is blush pink."

"It's just super weird."

"I'm sure picking today to get married was all about saving money. My aunt and uncle are pretty thrifty and they're paying for this wedding. They probably got a deal on the event space."

"I hope they got it for free."

"You didn't have to accept the invitation, you know," I say annoyed with her comments but mostly just annoyed period. "Cecily is my ridiculous cousin, but only I get to talk about her, not you."

"I had to accept. Would I leave my best friend to fend for herself in a den of vipers? You know your entire family is going be gunning for you for information about Jett. You're like a celebrity after that first article. Good thing you photograph well. Gossip sites have scrounged up pictures of you I haven't seen in years. Remember when I cut you those bangs in undergrad?"

"They can ask me all the questions they want to. There's nothing to talk about. I haven't talked to him in weeks."

"You can say his name."

"I'm fine."

"It's okay if you want to forgive him, A. In fact, I give you permission to forgive him. Hell, if it was me I'd give that fine human specimen a second chance, a third and a fourth."

"I'm going to blab to your husband how you're in here gushing over another man."

"Danny knows all about my celebrity crushes and he's perfectly fine with them because neither of us are going anywhere except back in bed with each other at the end of the night. That's the cool thing about marriage. "

I consider my behavior over the last few weeks. There hasn't been one day when I haven't thought about Jason, searched for news about him on the internet, or stared at my phone willing it to ring. Maybe the only person I'm punishing is myself.

I don't know.

I guess I'm waiting for some kind of sign to point me in the right direction or to help move past this man once and for all.

I just need a sign.

An hour later my hair has been expertly blown out and curled by Dena, but I still have another two hours before I have to go to my mom's to get my face done by the makeup artist she hired.

I click on the television and make my bed. The Nighthawks don't play until tonight, but I have recently learned that there are shows dedicated to the buildup to these games that are on all day. When I'm tucking in the corners of my sheets, I hear his name.

"As we do every Thanksgiving, we feature players who are not only excellent on the field but extraordinary human beings off it. This year our man of excellence feature is on Nighthawks Quarterback, Jason Jett Caraway."

I immediately turn up the volume and sit on the bed and watch.

"Jett caraway might just be one of the fastest and most accurate arms in the league, but he's also one of the most passionate about mental health, especially suicide prevention."

"Hi, Jett."

"Hey, Lou. Thanks for having me on."

"Yeah, man, so let's just jump in and talk about the work you do with your organization, Belief Village."

"Belief Village is a national non-profit organization which advocates for the mental health of people who are at most at risk for suicide in their communities. We pay for therapeutic counseling, medication, and other resources. We also provide an alternative to in-patient hospital treatment at our small ranch in Texas."

"I'd say it's a little more than a small ranch. You serve over 100 clients, every day, three-hundred and sixty-five days a week, right?"

"That's correct. We're very proud that we have the capability of serving so many people who normally might not have received appropriate mental health services in their community."

"And these are not just Texas residents."

"So far we are working with seven states. We hope to expand that reach as more funds become available to us."

"You'd also need a bigger ranch."

"Yeah," he grins.

God, I miss that smile.

"We'd probably need a bigger place."

"Jett, tell us what made you so passionate about the work that you do? This is a very particular focus on mental health and suicide prevention."

"Well, Lou, in the US alone, suicide is the tenth leading cause of death. Just last year, 47,511 people died by suicide. And the genuine tragedy is that we believe that we could have prevented many if not most of these deaths with strategic outreach at critical times.

"I became passionate about this cause after my mother, Gloria Caraway, committed suicide four well almost five years ago. There were periods during her battle with clinical depression that someone on her medical team should have advocated for her, but no one did. It's my mission to fix our broken mental health system one person at a time."

"That's so powerful, Jett. And your organization works with at-risk youth as well?"

"Oh, of course. The pressures on our young students are tremendous and growing with each year. When I was in school, I can think of several student athletes who could have really benefited from our services. The way our system works now, it's often the squeakiest wheel who gets the help. Many people fall through the cracks of the regular mental health system. I mean when was the last time the doctor at your well visit asked you how were coping emotionally?"

"Mmm, what a great point, and so fitting for the Thanksgiving Holiday. In honor and in the spirit of all that Belief Village does, Jett, the network would like to award you with this year's Spirit Award. In addition, we are donating twenty-five thousand dollars to your organization, which the NFL has promised to match. So a total of fifty-thousand dollars to continue the outstanding work you are doing."

"Thank you so much. This will help many people."

I am floored.

There are actual tears in the corner of my eyes.

I'm so ridiculously impressed and proud of what Jason is doing that I don't know what to do with myself right now. Why didn't I find any of this information during my snooping sessions? This interview filled in so many missing gaps about who he is that the gossipy online articles didn't.

He blames his mother's suicide on his father.

He probably was worried about me slipping into some sort of depression after Troy, which is why he spent so much time making me laugh.

He is not just a ballplayer who makes obscene amounts of money throwing a ball.

He is so much more than that.

I wish he could have shared all of this with me, but of course that would have blown his entire cover. He would have had to come up with a series of new lies to cover up the other lies, and deep down I know that's not who he is.

He's not a liar.

For the first time since this whole debacle occurred, I'm believing that staying under the radar may have initially been for his benefit but was good for mine as well.

Would I have even talked to him if I had known he was this larger-than-life sports celebrity? I don't think so. And I think he knew it too.

I look up toward the ceiling and crack a smile at God.

This was pretty obvious, even for you.

I asked for a sign and I got it.

I guess I better do something about it.

JETT

IT'S the Thanksgiving Day game and we're in Texas playing another one of our division rivals, Dallas. Although I'm several hours away from "home" I'm glad to be back in my home state where the air smells sweeter and familiar. There's always a bit of truth to the slogans that advertisers come up with. Everything is bigger and better in Texas.

I'm starting to understand what Coach T meant by not enjoying this stage of my recovery. My shoulder feels so much better than it has in weeks that I feel like with a little physical therapy I could definitely handle a few snaps. Of course, that's not how football works. You go with your quarterback for the whole game until you can't and right now that man is Rivera.

He hasn't been perfect this season, but he's been good enough to get us to this point with a good record. We have a fighting chance of getting a playoff spot, and winning this game would go a long way in getting us there.

There's a ferocity in the air as we jog into the bright lights of the 1.2 billion dollar stadium. I grab a headset so I'm able to communicate with the coaching staff and continue to familiarize myself with the game plays for the day. It's my job to watch the game and help Rivera make any adjustments if he needs to.

There are a few mild cheers as the offense gets started on our first play of the day. It's nice to see a few New Yorkers in the stands cheering us on. Our offense doesn't make it down to the red zone, but that's okay, they probably just need a little time to warm up and get their juices flowing.

By the third play, Rivera spots an opening and throws the ball to Gibson. It wasn't one of the planned offensive plays of the day, but that's the beauty of being a quarterback, it's our job to manage the game and change plays or make different plays if we see them. But Gibson doesn't see what Rivera is doing in time and runs completely the other way, and the football runs straight into the hands of the opposition.

It's an interception.

The guy runs the ball completely down the side of the field like his ass is on fire and no one can catch him.

It's a touchdown.

Their first of the day.

And it lights a fire under them.

The volume of the stadium increases by at least ten decibels and there's an energy in the air which blossoms that only a football player can understand. It's so thick that you could almost touch and squeeze it, but unfortunately it's in our opponent's favor.

Rivera walks back over to the bench and sits by me quietly while our defense takes the field. He's frustrated with the game so far, but mostly with himself.

Gibson walks over to where we're seated, totally furious.

"Are you blind? I was nowhere over there." He says to Rivera.

"You were supposed to cut left. Didn't you see what I was doing?" He defends himself.

"That wasn't even the play we were running."

"Whatever, man, let's just keep our heads in the game."

"No, you need to get your head into the game. I don't know what you're doing out there, but it ain't prime time football."

Tensions are high and a loss in Dallas would be denigrating for the city of New York, but I've never seen a player talk to Rivera like this. He's played long enough that he's owed a certain amount of respect and Gibson is stepping over the line, but I stay out of it. It's not my fight.

Rivera stands up and holds his ground, continuing to argue with Gibson. He refuses to take the blame for their miscommunication.

"Being able to make adjustments is part of prime time football, or didn't they teach you that at your rinky-dink university?"

Dayumm.

A couple other players on our offense come over and try to squash the beef, but it only makes the sidelines look like we are having a major quarrel. Television cameras love that shit and turn the focus of their cameras in our direction.

Something overcomes me when a lens points in my face. I guess because it's Thanksgiving, everyone's going home to their families after this game, and I haven't talked to Adrienne in so long that it hurts.

I miss the fuck out of her, but I finally realized that I needed to respect her wishes and give her the space that she asked for. That, and of course for her to actually miss me.

I'm addictive like that.

Eventually she's going to come around, and when she does, I'll be here.

I ain't going no fucking where.

Just in case she's watching, I face the camera and mouth words that are only for her.

I miss you, beautiful.

The second quarter of the game doesn't go too much better than the first. Our defense is doing their job, but our offense isn't putting any points on the board. Rivera hasn't found a groove and isn't connecting with any of our wide receivers. Gibson blames Rivera and maybe when you're in the middle of a game it feels that way, but now that I'm on the sidelines, I can see things a little differently. Gibson isn't running his routes like he's supposed to, and Rivera is off. I think his back hurts and he isn't telling anyone. His throws are just a little short and not as accurate as they've been in the past. During halftime, I tell the team what I see from my vantage point.

"I think we run the ball instead of going for the big touchdown pass every play. We do that, I think we can win this game. Rivera, just continue to hand off the ball to whoever is open like Taylor and Kennedy, and we might just win this thing one down at a time."

The coaches pat me on the back and tell me they appreciate my contribution. The plan for the second half of the game is to go in that direction and run the ball instead of always trying to throw it deep for the quick win.

I hang back for a moment when the team returns on the field. After I use the bathroom, something tells me to check my phone. It's in my locker. Electronics aren't allowed on the playing field during the game.

My instincts were right.

It's her.

It's not much.

Adrienne: Happy Thanksgiving

But I'll take it.

It's the opening I've been waiting for and wanting for months.

Me: Mac and Cheese or Yams?

Adrienne: Ham

Me: Still on your meat kick?

Adrienne: I'm like a carnivore now.

Fuck me.

Does she realize how sexy she is without even trying?

Me: I miss you, beautiful.

Adrienne: LOL, you said that already.

She was watching.

THIRTY-FIVE

JETT

AFTER THE GAME, I go back to the hotel and plan for a night of Thanksgiving room service and to catch up on some episodes of The Mandalorian. Many of my teammates are probably in the hotel bar or out at a local club celebrating, but I'm not in the mood. It's too late to catch a flight out to my ranch, and it makes little sense to go there, anyway. Thanksgiving is just not the same since my mother's death. For me, it's just another day. The only good thing about today is that Adrienne reached out to me. No, wait, that's a great thing.

I check in with Bryan before I settle in for the night.

"Good game."

"Yeah, Rivera looked good out there after halftime."

"Don't worry so much. He can't play another full season. His back is too unpredictable."

"She sent me a text today," I say like an excited schoolboy.

"That's progress."

"I think so too. So tell me, how is she?"

"She's fine. She works, she comes home, she studies, and then she gets up and does the same thing all over again."

"What about the ex?"

"Haven't seen a peep from him."

"He works at her hospital though."

"He works for the corporation that owns Mercy West. He doesn't even work in the same building. They never see each other."

"Can he sabotage her getting a permanent position there?"

"He's a financial grunt. He has no actual power. He can't do anything to her. If they want her to offer her a position, they will, and there's nothing he can do about it. And before you ask, there is no way you can force them to offer her a job after her residency is completed. You have no leverage in that world so fall back."

"Fine, but what's the deal with her friend Owen. Did you find anything out about him?"

"I'm not a private investigator, Jett."

"All I asked was a for a basic internet search on the dude. Come on, I know you did it."

"He's a doctor like she is. They went to medical school together. He's a resident at Mercy West too, but in the surgical unit."

"Oh, like Grey's Anatomy."

"Yeah, except for real."

"So, he's smart."

"Duh, he's a doctor."

"Does he have a girlfriend?"

"No."

That fucker.

"Can we get him one?"

"You need some sleep, Jett. We're not government operatives. I can't just put someone on him like Jason Bourne or 007."

"These aren't the answers I was looking for. You're making too much sense. I'm hanging up now."

"Happy Thanksgiving."

"Oh, crap, are you with your family right now?"

"Yep, we're about to play a round of Spades."

Shit.

"I'm sorry, man. Go be with your family."

"See you when you get back."

"Later, man."

A call comes in on my cell about fifteen minutes into my show and my tasty Hotel St. Germain Thanksgiving dinner; I'm surprised to see that it's my father. We rarely call each other and we definitely don't do pleasantries on holidays, so I imagine there must be a good reason for his call. That's the only reason why I pick it up.

"Hello?"

"Hey, Jett."

"Is everything okay?"

"Yes, everything's fine. I wanted to congratulate you on the win today and to wish you a Happy Thanksgiving."

"Thanks?"

"And I saw the segment the network did on you before the game. Congratulations on winning the Spirit

Award. That's a tremendous deal and a major accomplishment. I was real proud, son."

"Were you?" I say with contempt.

"Yes."

There's a loaded silence between us, and then he speaks again.

"How's the shoulder doing?"

"It's getting better."

"Do you think you'll get to play at the end of the season? Looks like you guys might get to play in the postseason."

"Why do you ask? Did you brag to buddies at work that I would play?"

He sighs. "Son, I wish you wouldn't be so angry with me. I'm just trying my best to have a decent conversation with you."

"And you know what I wish? I wish mom was still alive."

"You can't still blame me for your mother's illness, Jett."

"I'm going to win the Super Bowl this year or the next, and mom's going to miss it. She will never see me at my best."

"You were her crowning achievement, Son. She always saw you at your very best. I wish she was here too so that she could see all your successes, but that just wasn't what destiny had in store for her."

"I find that hard to believe."

"You find what hard to believe?"

"That you wish she were here."

"I didn't kill her, Jett!" He gets emotional but so do I.

"You might as well have shoved the pills down her throat yourself. You are the sole fucking reason why she was always so depressed, so despondent, so sad."

"You run a foundation that helps people like your mother. You should know that she was battling her illness way before she met me. I didn't cause it."

"You cheated on her constantly."

"I admit I made some mistakes."

"She stayed married to you and was miserable the entire time."

"Gloria was sick."

"And the minute she dies, you have the audacity to marry the woman you were cheating on her with. How could you ever think that I would be able to forgive that?"

"I didn't know anything about depression. I didn't know how to help her. I just knew that I would not leave you without a father. So we both stayed in the marriage and we were both miserable. We just didn't have the tools that your generation has now."

"The damage is done. I can't even have a real relationship because of the shit you pulled. I'm damaged goods. I'm too afraid I'm going to blow up some unsuspecting woman's life because of what I grew up seeing and you know what? I hate that about me!"

"I did the best I could. I raised you. I fed you. I went to as many games as work would allow me to. What do you want me to say, Jett?"

"And stop calling me Jett! That shit is weird. That's my football name. A name given to me by my high school football coach who actually gave a damn about me, not you. How do you just wake up one day and start calling your son Jett when I've always been Jason? Am I really just a fucking check to you?"

I hear a whooshing sound on the phone and then some other indescribable movement and then... tears. My father is actually crying on the phone.

Ugly crying.

I sit quietly on my hotel bed and listen to years of agony and guilt pour deep from his chest and his gut.

"I'm sorry, Jason."

Something about the revelation of his pain acts as a soothing balm for my own. It's exactly what I didn't know I needed.

An apology that was gut-wrenchingly honest.

I cry tears of my own for my mother, but these are different tears. I've finally gotten the apology she deserved to hear a long time ago, and I hope that wherever she is, her soul can finally rest knowing that mine is at peace as well.

I can't wait to share it with Adrienne.

Me: I talked some things through with my pop.

My phone immediately rings.

"Hey, beautiful."

"Are you all right?"

"I'm real good now that I hear your voice."

"Did you yell at him?"

"A little."

"Did he yell back?"

"A little."

"You blame him for your mother's suicide, don't you?"

"I think if he had been a better husband, she'd still be here with us."

"Do you feel better now that at least you've gotten some of that pain off your chest?"

"I do."

We both listen to the sounds of each other breathing.

"Adrienne."

"Yes?"

"You know my name. You know what I do for a living. You learned what I'm passionate about and the people I advocate for. You know I adored my mother and have complicated feelings for my father. You know I have a little sister who likes public television and could teach a manners course to her entire Kindergarten class. You know I don't like to take no for an answer. So I'm asking, is there anything else that you want or need to know?"

"What you want from me."

"A. Third. Fucking. Date."

There is complete silence between us. I don't know if I've pissed her off or if she fell asleep, but I wait. The ball is in her court. I've put it all out there. I know I fucked up, but I know I can do better. I just need her to give me the chance and if she does... then I've got it from there.

"When?"

YESSS!

"Christmas Eve. It's on a Thursday this year and we're going to start early, so I'll pick you up at four."

"I'll see you then."

"Dream about me tonight."

"Now you're pushing it," she chuckles.

When we hang up, I can't stop grinning. I'm not even

hungry anymore. I just slide into the cool white sheets of my King sized bed and dream about the best pussy I've ever tasted.

Adrienne's.

Needless to say, I get some of the best sleep of my life.

THIRTY-SIX

ADRIENNE

I'VE LEARNED some things about myself over the last few weeks and it hasn't been pretty. Are you ready to hear it? All I've done in the last four years is spend useless energy on the two sorry men I was involved with or study medicine.

That's it.

That's all.

The revelation came to me as I was filling out a profile for an online networking group (for Mercy West residents, of course). There was a section specifically for filling out my interests and hobbies, and I stared at the blank text box for ten minutes because I was stuck. I couldn't think of one thing interesting to list because I do nothing besides study or practice medicine.

It sounds like a very simple realization about oneself, but it was truly a profound moment for me.

I am one dimensional.

Boring.

Safe.

I am not taking the blame for Troy's vile behavior, but if I'm going to be truly honest with myself, then I'm kind of rethinking everything about that relationship. Perhaps he cheated on me and I completely missed it because our relationship was void of any real depth. We had only scratched the surface of each other, never peeling back any layers.

But things are going to be different from now on. I'm committed to broadening my horizons and expanding my reach. I want to know a little about a lot of things instead of my usual deep dive into one subject. I want to figure out who I am without the stethoscope. Who did Adrienne used to be before she settled with defining herself as the monolithic creature completely oblivious of the expansive world around her?

I figure the best place to start with is at the source.

Home.

"This is a pleasant surprise." Mom smiles when she opens the front door to let me in.

"Hey, mom."

"What's all that you have?"

"I thought we'd hang out today. I'm going to cook us a pot of mussels along with some garlic bread and we'll look at pictures of daddy."

I carry my bags of groceries straight through the living room and into the kitchen.

"I'll start cleaning the mussels."

"I'll go get the photo albums," she says excitedly.

I point to a picture I've probably seen a million times but ask my mother again, "Where was this one taken?"

"This was the day your father, and I drove to the mountains for your first week of overnight camp. We drove in one car and Lorraine and her crew drove in another." My mother remembers fondly. "You didn't want us to leave, so we spent the day helping you unpack and settle in. To help you adjust, Lorraine and I used our power of persuasion to get you and Cecily placed in the same cabin. For some reason, they made a mistake and had you two in separate cabins. You had the top bunk, and she had the bottom."

I distinctly remember that week of fresh hell. Cecily dominated all the girls in our cabin, telling us all what to do every moment of the day, and none of us were brave enough to stand up to her. Our parents described it as strong-willed. In today's society, Cecily would have been labeled a bully.

"Yeah, she almost drowned me that week." I admit out loud. I've never told my mother this story, but it's time I stop sheltering her from the truth. I can't pick my relatives, but that doesn't mean I have to like them. Cecily is, and has always been, an unlikable girl and I'm not sugarcoating it anymore.

"What do you mean?"

"We were at the lake and we were all being tested for how well we could swim. Each kid got a different color band based on your level. Red for beginners, yellow for can swim and float, green for strong swimmers who will be fine in the deep end of the lake on their own. Cecily didn't want that red string, so she lied and told the counselors that she could go in the deep end."

"And they listened to her?"

"Mom, most of those counselors were like nineteen years old, barely adults themselves, so yeah, they listened."

"That's true. They hired a lot of college kids. I forgot about that. So then what happened?"

"Cecily dove off the dock like she must have seen in a movie or something."

"Oh, my!"

"And then she sank right to the bottom."

"You never told me that story. Does Lorraine know?"

"I'm sure you would know about it if she told her mother."

"Why wouldn't she tell her mother that she almost drowned."

"She was embarrassed, Mom. Cecily's ego has always been too big for her body. I dove in after her because I knew the truth. I knew she couldn't swim a lick. I tried to save her, but she panicked and was pulling me down with her."

"Adrienne!"

"Luckily two of the senior counselors saw we were in distress, dove in, and saved us both."

"Did you get back in the water after that?"

"I swam all week. Cecily pretended like she didn't feel like getting wet and sat on the side of the lake sunbathing."

"You always did love the water, and Cecily never quite got the hang of it.

A spark of recognition goes off in my head.

I loved the water.

She's right.

"She also didn't speak to me the rest of that week. She was mad that I yelled at her in the water."

"Cecily?"

"Mom, I love our family and everyone in it, but Cecily is piece of work. She always has been."

After lunch, my mother kisses me on my cheek.

"You put your foot in that meal! Those mussels were delicious. Where did you learn how to make that white wine and butter sauce? It tasted like restaurant quality. So fresh."

"It's just something I whipped together. You can't go wrong with wine, garlic and butter."

"Mine never tastes that good. What are you coming over here next week to make?"

Another spark goes off.

I love to eat and I love to cook.

Of course I cook for survival, but it's been a while since I've actually cooked something new for the sheer enjoyment of it. Making my mom smile today by fixing her this lunch made me feel fantastic inside.

I need to do more of this.

I'd love to try cooking a five-course meal for Jason. He'd appreciate it more than anyone I know.

We end our afternoon watching the musical Dreamgirls (Beyonce version) and eating a bowl of popcorn with some old bay seasoning sprinkled on top. It kind of kept with the seafood theme of today's lunch and was really tasty.

When I leave to head back downtown, I feel ten pounds lighter. Sometimes in order for the tree to grow, you have to get back to the roots and figure out what were the things that made you thrive.

I remember now.

And guess what?

I'm awesome.

THIRTY-SEVEN

JETT

I HAVE A CONFESSION TO MAKE.

When I told Adrienne that I too preferred New Year's Eve over Christmas, I was sincere, but that's because I'd never had a Christmas in New York.

She was right.

There's nothing like it.

There's a vitality that you can feel among the people during the holidays in New York. Everyone is more optimistic, friendly, kinder, and just generally a happier person.

The city looks spectacular. There are lights everywhere. Every tree is adorned with strings of white lights, and they decorate many buildings with tasteful wreathes and festive lighting.

There are Santas on every other corner collecting change for the Red Cross. There are strangers singing for change in the subways and tourists in town to see the infamous Rockefeller center tree lighting.

There are Christmas concerts and restaurant nights and extended Christmas shopping hours.

The city is truly buzzing with Christmas spirit.

I've been preparing for this date for an entire month. It's been excruciatingly long, but the reality is that I knew we had a tough schedule of games ahead and that I wouldn't be able to give Adrienne my undivided attention.

Even though there are two more games of the regular season, at least we are going into this week knowing that we've won our division and cinched a spot in the playoffs.

Our next game is more important for the other team since our spot is assured, and will be played at home, so I'll be here for the entire week including Christmas.

Me: What time do you get off work today?

Adrienne: Three

Me: That doesn't give you much time to get pretty for me.

Adrienne: Lucky thing I don't need too much time then.

Me: Dress warm.

Adrienne. Where are we doing?

ME: Nice try. It's a surprise.

Adrienne: Didn't the contract say I get to pick a date?

Me: The second date, which you forfeited, so it's on me again.

Adrienne: I think you're making the rules up as we go along.

Me: Don't I always?

Bryan calls me to let me know that everything I've arranged is still good to go, and I can go pick Adrienne up whenever I'm ready.

"Just stick to the timetable."

"Okay."

"And good luck."

"No luck necessary, Padawan. I got this."

My driver pulls up in front of Adrienne's apartment and by a hydrant. One perk of having a driver is that you can have door-to-door service without the fuss. It's a pleasure I want Adrienne to be able to experience all the time now. I want to spoil her, sport her around town, give her everything she ever wanted. But I know I've got to take it one step at a time.

When I walk into the front door of the building, I notice a familiar figure coming out of the elevator.

I feel a sharp pain behind my left eye in my head.

It's tiny man and he could only be coming from one place.

We both stop a few feet away from each other and stare each other down. I don't understand why he's here, and I'm growing angrier with each passing moment.

His lips turn slightly up into a smug smirk. He's enjoying this.

"Congratulations," he says. "I haven't seen the Nighthawks play this well in a long time."

A jab to the fact that I'm not playing.

"What the fuck are you doing here?"

"Having a talk with Adrienne."

"About what?"

"That's between us."

"There's nothing between the two of you anymore."

"Is that what she told you?"

"That's what I know."

"Adrienne and I have a long history, Mr. Caraway. That doesn't just disappear overnight."

My head feels like it's about to explode. I straight on charge him with no regard to the consequences. It's as if I've totally forgotten that I've only got one good working arm. And then I wrap my hand around his tiny throat and squeeze.

"If I ever see you in this building again you will have a lot more to worry about then my hand around your throat. You will feel the weight of all of my influence on your life in a way that will feel suffocating. Kind of the way you feel right now."

I know that this man is probably thinking of ten ways he can sue me for everything I've got. That's what pussies like him do. But I don't give a shit.

All I know is that the need to protect what's mine has grown tenfold since I've met Adrienne. Since I've been inside of her. Since I've fallen in love with her. And make no mistake about it.

I protect what's mine.

"You're crazy!" he shouts. "Let me go."

"Remember what I said."

He nods his head in full understanding of what I told him.

"Ok, ok. I will."

I never want to see his ass anywhere near my girl again.

"Good."

I'm trying to calm down inside the elevator, but his words are fucking with me just like he intended them to. Just because we're going on this third date doesn't mean that Adrienne and I are on the same page.

I pound on the door like I'm a damn FBI agent.

Boof! Boof! Boof!

Calm down, man.

Remember the timeline.

You have no right to be this angry... yet.

She answers the door in nothing but a baby pink satin robe that hits the middle of her thighs and a smile on her face. I'm furious and turned on all at the same time.

"Why are you dressed like that?"

"And hello to you too."

"Why are you naked?"

"I just got out of the shower, Jason."

"Were you in that when he was here?"

"Who?

"Don't fucking play with me, Adrienne."

"What are you talking about?"

"I saw him."

"Who!?"

"Troy."

"Oh."

"That's all you've got as a response? Oh!?"

She giggles and turns around to walk away, but I grab her at the waist and pull her into my chest.

"Are you laughing at me?" I growl in her neck.

I can feel her heart beating quickly like a little rabbit. She's either lying or she's scared.

"You misunderstood, Jason."

"I misunderstood what?"

I slide my hand inside the opening of her robe and grab a full hold of her left breast. An audible moan escapes her throat.

"Did you let him touch you, Adrienne?"

"No," she whispers.

I pinch her nipple between my thumb and pointer finger and roll it back and forth. She leans all of her weight against me now, taking great pleasure in my touch.

I move my hand down and undo the small silk belt that holds the flimsy robe together. Once it falls, her robe opens and bares a freshly shorn pussy.

Fuck, I think my heart might explode.

I slide my hand through her folds and find that she is drenched with need.

"You're soaking wet, Adrienne. Is this for me or was that for him?"

I slide my fingers deftly inside of her fiery core and she gasps. "Are we still talking about him?"

"What have you done to me, beautiful?" I ask in a voice wracked with pain. I don't even recognize myself.

"Nothing," she promises.

I pull her with me towards the couch and turn her around to face me. I want to stare into her eyes when I ram my dick inside of her and claim her. I want to see the truth. Her eyes are wild with need. She wants me just as much as I want her. That's good.

"Unzip me," I order her.

She does what she's told like a good girl.

"Pull out my dick and put your mouth on it."

She fumbles a bit at first but pulls me out, scoots down to her knees and slides me into her mouth. My eyes roll back in my head for a moment as I succumb to the pleasure of having her warm lips around my cock. Before I come all over her pretty face or myself, I tell her to stop.

"Come ride this dick. It's been waiting for you for a long time. This time you're going to keep your eyes on your man the entire time. By the end of tonight, I'm going to be your every fucking thing."

She doesn't skip a beat. Her hunger for me is palpable. She climbs up on my lap, spreads her legs and positions herself above me. The sensation of me entering her tight, warm hole feels exquisite.

"Fuck, you're tight."

She stares at me with determination, and I stare back at her in wonder.

How could I have ever doubted her for even two-seconds? She's not a liar. This is Adrienne we're talking about. I see the truth in her eyes.

"Slowly, lower yourself, baby," I reassure her. "Take your time."

I wrap my lips around one of her nipples, which sends a rush of wetness to her core and helps her work the length and girth of me. She lowers herself inch by inch by excruciating inch, and it almost makes me want to howl like Astro does when the neighborhood's local firehouse alarm goes off.

I use my free hand to hold her to the side of her hip

and keep her steady as she works me up and down, back and forth.

And when she leans in to kiss me.

That's it.

She's got me now.

And I go crazy.

I lift her ass up with one hand and flip us both over on the couch, and I pound her pussy like I'm digging for gold. I stroke her deep and hard, and I hold her eyes with mine the entire time. It doesn't take long before she comes and I follow right behind her, saying her name on a prayer–*Adrienne*.

"Merry fucking Christmas," I say, totally satiated.

She giggles with a drunk kind of happy that I can feel in every cell of my body.

"Merry Christmas."

"I'm sorry for how I was acting at first. I wasn't myself."

"You said you saw Troy, but you didn't see him coming out of this apartment."

"Well, no, I saw him in the vestibule."

"That's because I found out that the woman he was cheating on me with lives in this building. That's why she thought he lived in this apartment."

"Damn."

"Yeah, damn."

"I don't know what he said to you downstairs, but he and I have not talked and have nothing else to say to each other. He has all his belongings. The landlord finally got around to changing my locks and that's that."

"Fuck, I'm embarrassed."

"So you're the jealous type, huh?"

"Only with you."

"Really?"

"Really."

"Should we get in the bed and make up some more? We could stay there all through Christmas."

I check the time.

"Shit, no."

"NO?"

"We've got things to do and your pretty ass just put us behind forty-five minutes." I pat her ass. "Get dressed."

"I'm going to need another shower, Jason."

"Make it quick or skip it. I'm only going to be back inside of you later."

"Ew, you're so nasty."

"Be honest with yourself, beautiful, I think that's why you like me."

THIRTY-EIGHT

ADRIENNE

THERE'S a dull ache pulsing between my legs as Jason and I sit in the backseat of his black Range Rover, holding hands and grinning like we've won some sort of jackpot.

It's a good ache.

The kind that reminds me I had no clue what satisfying sex was until I met him. In a very real way, I have truly hit the jackpot.

"I've been taking a cooking course online the last few days," I reveal, filling the quiet space with words other than medicine.

"What have you learned so far?"

"We're working on sauces. Did you know that the key to elevating any meal to restaurant level quality is by mastering sauces?"

"I certainly did not. I've got to say, Dr. Hodges, that I'm surprised you have time to be a gourmet chef, a pediatrician, and make me come."

He nuzzles my neck, and I chuckle with laughter.

"You are so bad."

"If it comes down to it and you have to make a choice out of the three, I hope you select correctly."

I slap his hand playfully.

"I'm making the time to do them all. I can't just be one thing anymore. It's not enough."

He nods quietly in understanding.

"I've decided that I will not hold Janet responsible for her parents' bad behavior."

"What do you mean?"

"Janet's mother, my father's wife, is the same woman he cheated on my mother with."

"How do you know that?"

"The timeline is too tight. He was definitely seeing her while still married to my mother because he married her less than a year after her death."

"It's possible to fall in love in a year." I say, only realizing how it may be interpreted until after the words leave my lips.

"That's true." He smiles and stares at me with those mesmerizing silver eyes of his.

"However they got together, it was the last straw for my mom. He was out, I was playing football, and she just couldn't handle it alone."

I clasp his hand tighter. I know this is difficult for him to talk about.

"She took a large dose of a mixture of Ambien and Valium, both of which had been prescribed to her by her primary doctor with no follow-up appointments or counseling. She had been gone half the night before anyone ever even knew."

"I'm so sorry, Jason. That must have been horrible for you."

I lift his hand to my mouth and kiss it.

"It was, and sometimes still is, because you know she died alone, but I think the conversation with my father helped me at least release some of my anger. Based on working within my organization, I know that she probably had been dealing with depression and anxiety for most of her life and that there could have been a variety of reasons why she ended her life that day. It was just easier to blame him."

"I can understand that, but like you said, Janet's a sweet child, and she adores you. It isn't fair to put her in the middle."

"Right, that's why I'm going to do better and pick her up more often. Maybe you can help me a little since you like kids."

"I can do that, and maybe we'd include your dad on some days."

"Uh, let's not get crazy, beautiful. He may not be Darth Vader, but he's still not my favorite person."

"Which bad guy is Vader again?"

"Don't tell me you didn't watch Star Wars growing up?"

"I was more of a hospital show kind of girl like Grey's Anatomy."

Jason squishes up his face in a weird.

"The one with all the surgeons?"

"Yeah, it's a great show."

"Your friend Owen's a surgeon, right?"

I crook my head to the side and give him a funny look.

"How do you know what kind of doctor Owen is?"

"I just assumed."

"The natural assumption would be that he's a pediatrician like me."

"You know you never told me what made you decide to become a pediatrician?"

"It was because of Kitty."

"Who's she?"

"She was a girl from my high school. She was quiet and studious and great at Algebra. We sat at lunch together, sometimes with a group of other students. What I didn't know for a long while was that she had been battling cancer for two years, which she finally succumbed to during our junior year."

"Damn."

"I spent the day with her once in the hospital and watched how her team of doctors diligently came in and out of her room, examining her and talking to her and the family. Then I remember seeing three of those same faces at her funeral. They truly gave a damn about her because I think for some doctors the work seems even much more important when you are saving a young life. A life that hasn't been lived yet."

I stare out the window thinking about Kitty when I notice our car is headed toward the City Hall area.

"I know where we're going."

"Do you?" He grins mischievously.

"The Brooklyn Bridge."

For a split second, I remember the feeling I had when little Brad Hines handed me that first bag of fruit chews.

I felt special.

And this feels even more special.

I turn and look at him adoringly in the eyes.

"You're sharing the Brooklyn Bridge View with me?"

"It's a little more than that, baby."

The car stops near the entrance of the bridge and parks in what is clearly marked as a tow-away zone, and we get out.

"We can't park here." I say pointing to the sign.

"It's fine. Can you just let me be romantic without you worrying about everything?"

The driver pops the trunk and Jason reaches in and pulls out a bouquet of flowers.

"Welcome to our third and final date."

Final? My heart sinks a bit. I don't like the sound of that.

"Thank you," I say graciously.

He grabs a picnic basket and his camera out of the car and the driver pulls out a few other bags and we walk.

"Let's go take our walk."

The first thing I noticed once we entered the pedestrian pathway of the bridge is that a police officer let us through a barrier that isn't normally there to enter and that there are no other people on the bridge.

"Is this the apocalypse?"

He chuckles. "Why do you ask that?"

"There are no people. I read somewhere that an

average of ten thousand people walk this bridge every day. Where are they?"

"I wanted to show you that everything about my celebrity and money are not bad things. I paid to have the pedestrian pathway closed to the public for three hours."

"Holy hell, you can do that?"

"If you pay enough money, yes."

"Do you still want to stay under the radar?" I ask, fearing the answer.

Is he embarrassed by me? That picture of me five years ago with the bangs wasn't the best.

"I want what's best for you and I think us taking things slow and steady and quiet is what's best while you are working towards your dreams. I don't want to be a disruption, but I also don't want to disappear from your life. I want to stick around if you'll have me."

We arrive to two tables set with white linens, flanked on both sides by two commercial sized, stainless steel patio heaters. One table is for all the goodies that the driver is pulling out of the gourmet grocery bags and the other table is seating for us.

"Thanks, Paul. You can head back."

"Enjoy your dinner."

Jason pulls out plates, cutlery and two well packaged meals of porterhouse steaks, grilled asparagus and lobster Mac and cheese.

My eyes widen with greedy delight.

"How did you know I liked lobster Mac and cheese?"

"I have my ways."

"You have a spy in my camp?"

"I bargained with Caroline. I told her if she got me

some intel on you, I'd allow her to use my photo along with my written testimonial."

"So Dena sold me out."

"Exactly."

"This looks really good, though. I may have to thank her."

"Let's eat while it's still hot. The steak is medium-rare just like you like it."

That damn Dena is a hopeless romantic and a snitch.

Jason uses his very expensive-looking camera to take multiple shots of the skyline and a few of me too. Then we watch in awe and delight as the sun sets and the city lights grow brighter with each passing moment. The two of us alone with the East River and city traffic rushing underneath us is almost surreal. It's the most romantic date I've ever been on.

"Are you warm enough, beautiful?"

"Yes, the heaters are great. How did you even get them on here?"

"I'm impressive, aren't I?" He grins.

"You are." I shake my head at his shameless ego.

"In all ways?" He raises his eyebrow suggestively.

"In every way."

"This is our third and final date under the contract, Adrienne."

"Uh-huh."

"But after this I'm hoping we'll begin a new contract."

I grin from ear to ear in relief. I wasn't sure what he was going to say.

"What do you have in mind?"

"If you don't answer, you're going to have to drink."

He hands me a shot glass and tears flood my eyes.

There's a shot of clear liquid with a huge princess cut diamond ring floating inside.

"Church wedding or elopement?"

THIRTY-NINE

ADRIENNE

"YOU DON'T HAVE to do this."

"I want to do this."

"Seriously, this is above and beyond the call of duty."

"If I didn't know better, I'd think you're trying to keep me hidden like I'm some sort of dirty little secret, Dr. Hodges."

Jason pecks me lightly on lips then rubs down his morning wood.

"Speaking of dirty."

It's Christmas morning and we're luxuriating in a sleek, king-sized bed that looks like it comes right out of a Modern Architecture magazine. Jason's two-floor penthouse is amazeballs. I mean, I've lived in this city my entire life and really didn't have a clue how the other half lived, but let me just tell you, the other half lives freakin' great.

I kiss him passionately this time.

"Yay, let's have Christmas sex!" I say excitedly.

He leans his head back.

"You don't want me to meet your family?"

"That's not true."

"The fuck it ain't."

"Why wouldn't I want my family to meet the most gorgeous, sexy and beloved man in sports?"

"Gorgeous and sexy, yes, but beloved? I'm the most hated man in football."

Several news channels picked up the feature done on Jason winning the Spirit Award and the publicity has given his career and Belief Village an enormous boost in recognition and popularity. The team has even talked to him about being prepared to play during the playoffs because of Josh Rivera's back, and he's been getting aggressive physical therapy in preparation.

"Not anymore."

"Okay, well your family hasn't seen me in the flesh, so they don't know what an amazing man you've got. They need to see and touch me for me to be believed."

"You're insufferable. I don't think I truly realized how inflated your ego is."

"Inflated or accurate, darlin'?"

Jason's pet Rottweiler, Astro, butts the bedroom door open with his head and strolls inside. He places his chin on the edge of the bed and stares lovingly at his daddy.

"He's so cute. Does he always greet you like this in the morning?"

"This isn't him greeting me. This is him running from Mittens."

After our private picnic under the stars, we stopped

at my place to pick up some extra clothes, my laptop, some kitty litter and my cat. There was no way I was going to spend Christmas without her. It never dawned on me that Astro might not like that arrangement.

"Astro doesn't like cats?"

"We don't have any at the ranch."

"What ranch doesn't have cats?"

"Mine."

"Cats keep away mice."

"The mice stay in the fields or in the chicken coops."

"This is a disaster."

"They'll figure it out."

"Should we keep them separated for now? Will he hurt her?"

"I'm offended. Astro's been nothing but a gentleman, as am I."

I lay across Jason's body and rub the top of Astro's head.

"You're right. He's adorable."

"God, your ass is perfect."

"How's your shoulder doing? Are you in any pain?"

The bandage wrap has been off of Jason for about four days, which is both a good and bad thing. It's great because that means he's healing, but it also makes him think that he's better than he really is. His bones are not completely healed yet. He still needs to be careful.

"I'm great."

"Are you sure?"

I gently smooth my fingertips across the area.

"I could prove it to you in a hundred different ways in my shower right now. There are four shower heads in there and it'll feel like I'm fucking you under a waterfall."

"No, thank you."

"You just wanted to have sex with me two minutes ago."

"Safely, in this marvelous bed."

"I thought you wanted to broaden your horizons. I'll lift your ass up in my hands and fuck you properly against the marble. Your feet will never touch the floor."

"We tried three unique positions last night I've never even heard of. I think I broadened my horizons enough for this year. Let's save something for the honeymoon."

He laughs heartily and smacks my ass.

"Get up I want to show you something," he tells me.

He tosses me a Nighthawks jersey to put on. It's black and gold with a number seven on it and hangs like a dress on me. I follow him in bare feet and greet Mittens in the hallway.

"Hi, girl." I lift her up in my arms and carry her with me to wherever we're going. "Did you sleep well?"

"What sleep? She was stalking poor Astro all night."

"She's predatory by nature. That's why I don't have any mice in my apartment."

"Whatever, enabler."

We walk inside another closed room and the first thing I notice are all the windows. The spectacular view overlooks the Eastside of the city, and I can see why he brought me here. He has several easels set up with works in progress, including a sunset view of New York from the Brooklyn Bridge.

"Wow, this is your studio."

"You could call it that. It's my happy place."

"I love it."

He walks over to a painting that is covered with a large painter's cloth. When he lifts it, I recognize myself. It's a nude oil painting of me, sleeping on my side, with a smile on my face. It's a gorgeous likeness, and it doesn't escape me, it's how Jason must see me.

As beautiful.

"When did you do this?"

"I painted this from memory after the first night we were together. I knew then that you were something special, and I had to capture it on canvas."

"You made me look really... pretty."

"I told you I see you for who you really are, Adrienne, and I will spend the rest of our lives showing you who that woman is. She's a healer. She's a boss bitch. She's the most beautiful woman in the room."

I silently blush.

Jason is my biggest cheerleader ever. He makes me feel so beautiful.

"Now let's get dressed. We can wrap this up as a gift to your mom."

"Jason!"

"You're so damn gullible, of course I will not gift your mother a naked picture of her daughter to her. Then she'll know I banged it out before the wedding night!"

"Oh my God, we aren't going."

"Oh, we're going. Your mother has the right to meet the man her daughter is going to marry."

"Does it have to be today?"

"To-fucking-day."

I grew up enjoying Thanksgiving dinner over different family member's homes. Sometimes we were with my mom's side of the family and other years we were with my dad's, but Christmas is different. Christmas has always belonged to mom and Aunt Lorraine. They love it. Which means that many of my mom's side of the family will be there. Many of whom have zero filter or celebrity manners.

"I think I should prep you first... or them for you."

"All moms love me. I've got this."

"It's not just my mom."

My first thought is Cecily. I guarantee it will be her sole mission to passive-aggressively embarrass me in front of Jason.

"Go get dressed. I put your things in the second drawer of the chest in my bedroom."

"You put my things in a drawer?" I ask incredulously.

"Yeah."

"But I'm going home tonight, Jason."

He slides his tongue in between my lips and leisurely makes love to my mouth for a moment.

"Who says you are?" he whispers into my skin.

Holy shit.

This has got to be love.

FORTY

ADRIENNE

I WASN'T A COMPLETE FOOL.

I took my cell phone with me into Jason's bathroom and called my mom ASAP. There was no way I was walking into Christmas Dinner without giving her a heads up.

"Mom," I whisper.

"Merry Christmas, Sweetie!"

"Merry Christmas. Listen, I'm bringing a guest to dinner."

"That's fine. Who are you bringing?"

I stare at the gorgeous new rock on my ring finger but don't dare tell her about the engagement yet.

"My, um, boyfriend."

"Troy?"

"Mom."

"The football player?"

"Yes, Ma."

"Goodness, if I had known he was coming I would have made some extra dishes."

"The normal Williams Christmas is fine."

Williams is my mom's maiden name and it will be her twin sister, their first cousins (all women), Cecily, plus a few husbands at dinner.

"Why wouldn't you tell me before this, Adrienne?"

"It was a last-minute decision. Do you want to meet him or not?"

"Of course I do."

"Then we'll be there tonight for dinner. I'm just letting you know."

"Maybe there's time to make a shrimp cocktail."

"Mom, listen to me, don't do anything extra, just keep the troops in line."

"Well, we've never had a celebrity over for Christmas dinner. There's bound to be some excitement."

"Okay, mom." I give up. "I'll see you at six-ish."

I'm not sure that conversation went the way I hoped it would, but I'm just going to hope for the best and pray that my family doesn't scare away the best thing that has ever happened to me.

"You just couldn't help yourself, could you?"

Jason startles me with the deep bass in his voice.

"She needed to know there'd be one more for dinner."

He slides some of my hair out of my face.

"Let me give you a bath and settle you right down."

He always knows what to say to put a smile on my face.

"Yeah?"

"Yeah."

Jason draws a warm bath in his sunken jacuzzi and helps me in. He uses a sea sponge and pours a good amount of some fancy body wash on it and rubs it all over. He washes me by starting at my neck, to my arms, then my shoulders, my breasts, my stomach, and then finally uses additional pressure to slide the sponge between my legs. My head drops back against the base of the tub as he slowly and methodically cleans between my legs.

"Does this feel good, baby?"

"Oh, yes."

"Shit, you're already quivering."

I swallow thickly as an orgasm coils around my spine and settles in my core.

"This is a greedy pussy. She wants all my time and attention."

I nod shamelessly.

"She does."

"Then I guess I better give it to her."

Jason slides opposite me into the jacuzzi in his boxer briefs, lifts my legs onto his shoulders, and devours me ravenously. The orgasm hits me fast, hard and straight to the back of my head. I see stars.

"Jason!"

He lowers me back down in the water as I come down from my orgasmic high.

"Open your eyes, beautiful."

I do as I'm told.

I'll do whatever this man tells me to.

"I love you," he says irrefutably.

"I love you too."

"Good, I'm going to take a shower now."

"Okay," I say dumbstruck.

He kisses my mouth gently and climbs out of the tub. Then he peels off his soaked boxer briefs and enters his walk-in shower. His eyes are trained on me as all four of his shower heads turn on and stream hot water all over his massively beautiful body. He finally turns away from me and leans his body against the shower wall, allowing the water to his shoulder and his back.

Seeing his ink and his physique from this angle, through the glass doors, makes him look like a work of art. My ovaries immediately send a direct message to all the nerve endings in my body.

Make babies with this man.

Hell, I'm practically drooling.

I can't believe he's mine.

"Adrienne."

"Yes?"

"I told you to finish up."

Yes, sir.

If I thought I felt stupid gawking at my brand new fiancé as he took a shower in front of me today, imagine how I feel as several Williams women silently make bedroom eyes at him throughout dinner. These women have never been this quiet in my life. The men at the table are no better either.

"This ham is delicious, Mrs. Hodges." Jason compliments my mother's cooking.

"Thank you, it used to be one of Adrienne's favorites."

"It still is mom."

Cecily hasn't said a peep but has been glaring at me for the last hour. On the other hand, her husband has been chomping at the bit to talk to him ever since we arrived.

"So, Jett, the news says you may come back for the playoffs. I play in a fantasy league and it might be good to get some insider info."

Seriously?

"I'm still on the injured reserve list, but I'll be ready if anything happens to Rivera."

"That's good to hear. You were a phenom in college, by the way. I followed you big time when you were at Penn State."

"Thanks, man."

Dinner continues to be awkwardly polite but relatively manageable until Jason looks at my hand. I still have on my ring, but the band is turned around so that the diamond is facing the inside of my hand.

"We'll have to get this resized."

He grabs my finger and turns it around so that the diamond shows. It sits high and bright and reflects the light of the chandelier into what looks like a million little sunbeams.

"Whoa, Adrienne!" my Aunt Lorraine exclaims. "Are you trying to blind us with that ring?"

"Ring?" Half the table says in unison.

My entire family whips their heads over to focus their attention on my finger.

"Are you engaged?" Cecily asks incredulously.

My mother's face turns a shade of gray. She hates being the last to know anything, and I realize I must have disappointed her. I knew I should have prepped her better than this.

"It just happened," I try explaining myself.

"It must have *just* happened," she says. "You haven't been dating that long, have you?"

"I'm the luckiest guy, aren't I?" Jason says to break the tension. "I asked her last night, and she thankfully said yes."

"I'd say that Adrienne is the lucky one," Cecily interjects with a bitter intonation. "Two engagements in one year? You must have a snapper between those legs."

I stand straight up from the table and my chair falls back on the floor with a loud crash.

That's it.

I'm sick of her shit.

I slam my fist on the tabletop and stare her down fiercely.

"What the hell did you just say?"

"I'm just saying what everyone is thinking."

"You no class bitch!"

My entire family stands up and tries calming us down, especially our mothers. Jason is visibly angry, but I can tell he's holding back for my sake. The last thing I need for him to do is to overreact in defense of me. I need to fight my own battle this time.

I touch his hand as a signal to stand down.

"Maybe this one won't dump you," Cecily spits.

"Cecily, that's enough of that." My Uncle Bobby, Cecily's dad, finally speaks up, albeit ineffectively.

"I should have let you drown," I tell her.

"Adrienne!" My mother reprimands.

I know, that was low, even for me.

"Are you talking about summer camp?" She guffaws. "You've always hated me, haven't you? You know I didn't want to put you in the wedding but Mommy made me."

"You think I wanted to be in that ridiculous blush pink Thanksgiving Day wedding?"

"Adrienne," Jason grabs my hand because I'm visibly shaking with rage.

"This is why I didn't want to come.," I say to him in a shrill voice. "Do you see?"

"You've always thought you were better than me, even back then," Cecily continues berating me.

"I am."

She didn't expect that response and is quieted by my confidence and Jason's silent but strong support of me. Of course I ruined dinner, but the look on her face was frankly worth it.

"Lorraine? Can you come here for a moment?"

My mother pulls her twin sister to the side, and they have a brief conversation. Their mannerisms are almost identical and their facial expressions are somber. I don't know what exact words were exchanged between them, but they hugged afterwards and then suddenly Aunt Lorraine announced it was time for everyone to leave.

"Do you want to go too, baby?" Jason whispers in my ear.

My mother speaks before I can answer.

"I'd like for you to stay so we can get to know Jett better."

"You can call me Jason, Mrs. Hodges," he tells her with his signature hundred-watt smile.

"Then, Jason, please stay and you can call me mom."

My mother pulls me in for a long hug, and whispers in my ear, "I like him and more importantly I think he loves you."

I grin and whisper back, "I hope so, because I'm head over heels for him."

After the three of us finish our dinner and splurge on a slice of apple crumb cake, my mom asks if we feel up to staying a little longer. Jason is of course happy to stay. He's working so hard to win her over after Cecily and I basically ruined Christmas.

"Movie or photo albums?" I ask him.

"That sounds like a trick question," he replies.

"If you don't make a choice, you have to drink."

"You know I'm not drinking any alcohol right now."

He's back on his strict eating and exercise regimen to get back in shape for football.

"Sorry, but that's how the game is played. If you don't want to mess up your diet, then you should just answer the question."

He looks between both me and my mother and finally gives an answer.

"Photo albums."

My mother claps a single time with approval.

"Great choice! I'll go get them. You two get comfortable."

After my mom is out of earshot Jason comments, "So, um, I see why you picked elopement."

"We should have hung out with my Dena and Danny," I chuckle.

"That cousin of yours is a piece of work."

"Did you want to slap her?"

"I don't hit women, darlin'."

"But if you did, you'd want to slap her, wouldn't you?"

He chuckles lightly.

"No, but I almost thought you were going to."

"You knew my mom wanted to look at the photos instead of a movie, didn't you?"

"I think she wants to introduce me to your father and I can't wait to meet him."

I give him a chaste kiss on his lips.

"Thank you. I knew I didn't walk into The Wild Boar for nothing."

"Your father sent you there to meet me. It wasn't an accident."

I kiss him a little longer this time.

"You are amazing, Jason Jett Caraway."

"I know, beautiful, that's what I've been trying to tell you for months."

AFTER HIM

ADRIENNE

I AM A FORTUNATE WOMAN.

All my hard work has finally paid off, and I've just
been offered a permanent position as a physician in the
Mercy West Pediatric Clinic. I remember when my
father bought me my first toy doctor's kit. My bedroom
was the hospital, my Barbie dolls were the patients, and
I'd play in my room for hours. I pray that wherever he is,
he's watching and he's proud. It's a dream come true.

Another cool thing? Our clinic now works closely
with Jason's organization, Belief Village, in administering
one of their suicide prevention screenings to help identify
at-risk patients in our practice.

My mother and I now spend two nights a month
researching and cooking new recipes together, and we try
to plan one of those nights when Jason is in town and

available for dinner because my man loves to eat just as much as I love to cook for him.

Jason never got the chance to play in last season's playoff game (which they lost), but the good news is that his shoulder is totally healed and he's back as the starting quarterback of the team. He's been giving me weekly lessons on the rules of the game, so that I can better understand it and eventually like it, but it doesn't mean that I don't flinch every single time he throws the ball and I watch all of those huge men whose sole goal is to "sack" the quarterback.

"I rarely get sacked, beautiful. I'm too fast. That's why they call me Jett."

"Quiet, I'm telling my version of the story."

The universe kept trying to teach me the lessons I needed to learn in order to grow as a woman and help me arrive to this place in my life but I continued to fail the test.

The truth was, Jason was right. I did have a list. It may not have been written down but it was in my head and it influenced all of my bad decisions. Even when a small part of me knew that my relationships weren't quite working, I put my Kindergarten Adrienne blinders on and saw what I wanted to see. I romanticized them like the perfect couples in all of the movies Mom and I watch.

What I was missing was the belief that I was good enough for someone like Jason: raw, honest, and more romantic than any rom-com protagonist could ever be. How ironic that it was that this man I thought had none of the qualities on my "list" was put in my life to teach me what love should really look like and that I was worthy of it.

Yes, the greatest fortune I've found is not one that every woman is lucky enough to find in a lifetime: Unconditional love + mind-blowing sex + unflappable trust.

And he also just happens to be a great quarterback.

"Wait, what?"

"The best player that ever lived."

"That's better, beautiful. Just remember to say that when we record Caroline's video testimonial afterwards."

"After what?"

"You strip."

Thank you for reading Jett (Jason) and Adrienne's story. Get ready for the next Nighthawk hottie's story available now.

RUSH is a new and angsty **friends-to-lovers**, football romance, between a strong and steamy NFL tight end and his carefree best friend. They might just be the perfect match if only they could get out of their own way.
DOWNLOAD NOW

69
RUSH
LISA LANG
BLAKENEY

THE BONUS EPILOGUE

Want to know what Jett and Adrienne are doing in the future?
GET THE BONUS INSTANTLY

You can find all my extra bonuses here.
https://lisalangblakeney.com/private-ninja-room/

RUSH SNEAK PEEK!

University Of Miami

There's something about the golden crackle of an enormous bonfire that I'm drawn to yet also frightens me. Perhaps it's the dazzling flicker of the flames or the powerful feeling that grows inside my chest as I watch the luminous flames grow in height with each log thrown on the pyre. Something about it seems so ominous.

Maybe in a past life I was a witch who danced in the moonlight in nothing but her birthday suit, but tonight I dance with all of my teammates around the flames in joyful anticipation of our playoff game tomorrow against our rival, Florida State.

It's so much fun to let loose after two weeks of intense preparation for one of the most important volleyball games of our lives. Not only do we want to win, but there will be a scout at the game for the US Olympic team and playing in the Olympics has always been my dream.

"You're like a Wiccan minus the flowy white dress spinning around the fire like that."

I spread my arms even wider as I twirl around the bonfire in my bare feet, laughing boisterously at my teammate, Pearl.

"You know I love to dance. This is the best stress reliever before a big game."

I grow dizzy and almost fall to the moist Miami sand beneath my feet when my best friend, Rush, catches me just in the knick of time.

"Gotcha."

I grin goofily when I see his stern face looking down at me while many of the other girls around the fire swoon. Rush is a big deal at our university. He plays tight end for the Hurricanes and is one of the more popular players to fantasize about.

"All those nights at the gym are paying off," I say impressed. "You caught me with one arm and it's not even shaking."

Pearl plops herself into the sand and gawks at my unassuming friend like most girls do here at school whenever Rush is around.

"You're going to break your neck one day," he fusses. "Where are your sneakers?"

"Ha, you sound like my *paw-paw*."

"You need to be careful. You could step on a cracked seashell or a freakin' beer bottle and put a hole in your foot. Then there'll be no playoff game in your future."

I ignore my curmudgeon of a friend. He's a worrier by nature and isn't the best with social graces and niceties, but I know he means well.

"Isn't the fire magnificent?" I ask him.

"Yes, yes, the fire is big," he answers dismissively.

"I can totally feel my ancestors sending me bountiful vibes tonight, Rush. We're going to kill it tomorrow. We're going to crush Florida State!" I say loud enough for everyone to hear.

"Yeah!!" My teammates collectively holler back. "Woo-hoo!"

"Of course you're going to win," Rush affirms. "You're the best team in the region."

"You're going to be at the game, right?"

"I have my own game to get ready for. I have to practice."

"Rush Bacchetti! I can't believe you."

"What do you want me to do, Mia? You know coach doesn't make exceptions about practice, even when it comes to you. He'll bench me if I don't show up."

I met Rush my freshman year. While we were both recruited to the university on athletic scholarships, let's just say he has always been a lot more precious to the college than I ever was. Football players are like gods to this place and are treated as such. It only took me a second to understand the athletic hierarchy once I stepped inside the football team's athletic dorm. It was like a damn Four Seasons Hotel compared to our accommodations, which looked more like a tidy Motel 6.

I was invited over by another ballplayer, an older sophomore, who probably wanted to get inside my pants that day, but once I started raising hell about the differences in the dorms and the privilege I was seeing (like free vending machines for them while ours were coin-operated), he was completely turned off. He shook his head and walked away, wanting no parts of my equality for all hissy fit.

Rush, on the other hand, was interested.

"What's wrong with your dorm?" he asked, genuinely curious.

"Do you want to see the hovel they've got the volleyball queens of this university staying in?"

"Sure, I'm down."

From that moment forward, the two of us became friends and kindred spirits. We would grab lunch often and go to each other's games for support. We'd often sit on campus and talk about our favorite classes or our least favorite professors. We were an unlikely pair; sort of like The Odd Couple. He was quiet and focused, and I was bubbly and all over the place. He came from a solid two parent family and I was from an emotionally unavailable single mom. He seemed to ace his classes with little effort, and I had to study throughout the night just to pass a chapter quiz. He held people at a distance and I always gave people too much credit, but something about our friendship works.

People have never understood it, but I'm smart enough to know that you don't meet many people like Rush in a lifetime which is why I have always valued our friendship and definitely depend on it. And while I'd never say this out loud, because I know it would make him feel guilty, it makes me nervous that Rush won't be at one of the most important games of my career.

He's my good luck charm.

When Rush comes to our games, I know there will be lots of loud claps and cheers for us because when anyone from the football team attends our matches; the groupies are sure to follow. That means we'll have a large crowd of spectators, which is always fuel for an athlete's motivation. More importantly though, Rush is my biggest fan. If he's not going to be there tomorrow, it will feel like an essential part of the team will be missing.

I grab a bottle of 100% cranberry juice out of the cooler of beer and hand it to him.

"You thirsty?"

"Wow, I thought, there'd only be beer here. You volleyball chicks are drunks."

"You know I wouldn't forget that you're the most *disciplined* football player in the entire university, so I bought you some juice."

He knows that using disciplined is my code word for describing how regrettably predictable he is. Throughout our years here on campus, he's been known to be the fun police. He's pulled me away from more frat parties than I care to remember and away from school clubs that in his words "were nothing but a distraction".

"Only the disciplined players get into the pros, Bird."

"I know, I know, but you only live once and if I want to drink a beer before the game, I'm going to have one. It ain't going to kill me," I retort. "I'm sure plenty of Olympians drink a beer or two."

"Why do you call her Bird?" Pearl asks Rush with the goofiest grin across her face. I forgot she was even there for a moment.

"She sings all the damn time," he tells her.

"Just like a bird," I say, imitating one by flapping my arms as if they were wings.

One of my other teammates changes the song on the portable bluetooth speaker and it's a Black Eyed Peas classic. I can't help myself and start dancing around the bonfire like a possessed woman.

"You can't possibly be drunk yet," Pearl comments, laughing at my dance.

"She's not," Rush tells her. "That's her totally sober."

"I drink beer because I genuinely enjoy the taste and not because of any way it may alter my state. A girl like me is drunk on life."

Everything I said was true. Regardless of my crappy home life, I'm just a genuinely cheerful person. I was born that way.

I stop in front of Rush and try mimicking a dance I saw a little boy doing in a viral video. I do it because he thought the video was just as hysterical as I did.

"Seriously?" He cracks a smile and slides his hand through his thick mane of chestnut-colored hair. "You look like a zombie in a hip hop dance class."

"This song reminds me of the sixth grade," I say as I continue to exuberantly dance. "My Grandmom bought me the album and didn't pay attention to the parental warnings. She just assumed they were a squeaky clean group."

"Rookie Grandmom mistake."

"Yep, it was awesome!"

I pump my fists to the rhythmic beat of *Boom Boom*

Pow as Rush sinks down to the Florida sand and watches me in complete wonder.

"You're going to be completely wiped for the game if you keep this up."

"Never!" I say, panting. "Remember, Bacchetti, I won our last two mile race."

"I gave you a head start."

"Not by much!"

My favorite part of the song comes on and I start pop locking my joints like I'm in a 1980s hip-hop video.

"Damn, you're like the energizer bunny," Pearl comments.

"Did your parents tell you about MTV when they were young?" I ask them, slightly out of breath. "It was like the only place they could see their favorite artists perform when they were kids. Isn't that nuts?"

"My parents didn't watch cable," Pearl says.

"Rush?" He doesn't answer at first. "Isn't that wild?"

"Yeah, yeah," he finally replies, totally ignoring me now and paying more attention to the texts coming in on his phone.

"Who's that?" I ask him.

"Kayla."

"Ooh, that's the pretty girl from California in the school of business, right?"

"Yeah."

"She sending you dirty texts?"

"Nah, Bird, she's not like that."

"I bet." I give him the side eye.

All girls are like *that* when it comes to Rush. I once

saw a girl wait forty-five minutes to say hello and hand him a greeting card on Valentine's Day. It was the cutest yet saddest thing I've ever seen. Rush prefers words over cards. He thinks greeting cards are a waste of money.

After the song ends, I plop down next to him totally exhausted yet oddly invigorated.

"Whew!"

"Gross, you're sweating."

He pushes my head off of his shoulder.

"It's the heat of my ancestors calling to me."

"It's because you were jumping around like your pants were on fire."

"It's called dancing."

"If that's what you want to call that. You've got like fifteen more minutes and then we need to leave. I've got curfew and so do you last time I checked."

"Alright, *paw-paw*." Then I stand again. "But just one more dance."

***

On game day, I complete all of my usual rituals. I brush my teeth for exactly four minutes. I wear my lucky pair of sunshine yellow panties. I lay naked on my bed for exactly ten minutes and meditate with four crystals in the center of my chest. And finally, I make my pre-game phone call between me and Rush.

The call is even more important today because I know I won't get to see his scowling face in the stands. When he calls, he only has to say a few words. I know what they mean. We've been saying them to each other since we met freshman year.

"World domination greetings, Mia."

"World domination greetings, Rush."

"Talk to you after you beat their asses?"

"Affirmative."

Then we hang up, and all is right with the world.

This game is going to be epic.

***

Your life can change in moments... even seconds, and no one ever told me. I probably wouldn't have believed them if they had.

Our game against our conference rival is going fantastically as we knew it would. Our team is stronger and faster and we have insane chemistry, but as I leap high to spike the ball like I have a million times before, my left ankle buckles when I land.

Then my left knee pops.

And then the most intense pain radiates throughout my body.

And I cry out for God.

I already know what I've done. I'm in my senior year of physical therapy school. I've completely torn my ACL. No doctor has to tell me. I can feel it. It's the injury every athlete most fears.

The small crowd of spectators grows quiet as I lay in the sand writhing in pain and watching my entire future disintegrate before my eyes. The smoke and ashes of a promising Olympic career, up in flames just like the beautiful bonfire I attended last night.

I'll have to go back home to Philly.

To a mother who won't be happy to have another mouth to feed in her home.

Even worse, I'll be going back to a life of musicless, colorless, cold mediocrity.

And for me, that's no life at all.

Ready To Find Out What Happens Next?
DOWNLOAD RUSH NOW

THE NIGHTHAWKS

Have you read all of the books in the scorching hot Nighthawk Series? Each novel features an alpha hot baller and a happily ever after:)

Saint - Saint & Sabrina
Wolf - Cooper & Ursula
Diesel - Mason & Olivia
Jett - Jett & Adrienne
Rush - Rush & Mia
Freak - Freak & Willow
Brick - coming soon!

ACKNOWLEDGMENTS

I want to send a huge thank you to my small and mighty team of friends and family who have been my rock through a difficult year.

I also want to send a huge thank you to my fierce romance ninjas who support all of my books and spread the word like the awesome LLB evangelists that they are! You all rock!

*A special shout out goes to romance ninja, Cheryl Griem, for helping me name Jett's dog, Astro. It was the perfect name:)

WHERE YOU CAN FIND ME

MY VIP LIST (Get the nitty gritty)
I have a VIP Reader mailing list. I only send free books, new release, sales or special giveaway information to this group. No spam. You can join here:
http://LisaLangBlakeney.com/VIP

MY PRIVATE FAN GROUP (Casual fun)
Join my private Fan Group on Facebook also known as my "Romance Ninja Warriors" where I share all things new going on, celebrate birthdays, post teasers, yummy pics, giveaways and just chit chat.
http://LisaLangBlakeney.com/community

THE ARC TEAM (Book Reviewers)
If you are interested in joining my beta reader team then please join here: https://geni.us/N8jAU

The King Brothers Series

Dive into this series of interconnected standalones featuring 3 alpha hot brothers and the women they lay claim to without apology.

Claimed - Camden & Jade
Indebted - Cutter & Sloan
Broken - Stone & Tiny
Promised - All King Brothers
King Brothers Box Set

The Nighthawk Series

Sexy & sweet sports romances set in the professional world of football. All standalones.

Saint - Saint & Sabrina
Wolf - Cooper & Ursula
Diesel - Mason & Olivia
Jett - Jett & Adrienne
Rush - Rush & Mia
Freak - Freak & Willow
Brick - Brick & Kaya
Dak - Coming soon

ABOUT THE AUTHOR

Lisa Lang Blakeney is a USA Today Bestselling author of contemporary romance sold in more than 28 countries. Worried that her fellow PTO moms might disapprove, she wrote and published her steamy debut novel Masterson under a different title and pen name in August of 2015.

Thanks to strong reader support of her alpha male character, Roman Masterson, she was encouraged to continue with the series and published the entire Masterson Trilogy the following year. She hasn't looked back since and continues to write novels featuring strong alpha men and the smart women they seek to claim.

A romance junkie for sure, you can find Lisa watching a romantic comedy, reading a romance novel, or writing one of her own most days of the week. If she's not doing that, she's outside in the garden tending to her roses.

Lisa is the wife of one alpha (whom she met in college), mother to four girls, and two labradoodles. Get news on releases, sales and giveaways when you become one of Lisa's VIP readers at : http://LisaLangBlakeney.com/VIP

facebook.com/authorlisalangblakeney

twitter.com/LisaLangWrites

instagram.com/LisaLangBlakeney

amazon.com/author/lisalangblakeney

bookbub.com/authors/lisa-lang-blakeney

goodreads.com/Lisa_Lang_Blakeney

pinterest.com/lisalangwrites

tiktok.com/@lisalangblakeney

patreon.com/lisalangblakeney